TAKE CARE

MONIQUE FISHER

TAKE CARE

1

JAMILA

Jamila carefully applies the metallic lavender eyeshadow to Daisy's eyelids. She makes sure to take her time. Daisy's nervous enough as it is, so the last thing Jamila wants is for her to be anxious about her makeup.

Daisy's violet eyes are currently filled with terror. Being one of the newest hires at the Kitten Heel Cabaret, Jamila has taken Daisy under her wing. Tonight is her stage debut and Jamila insisted on helping her get ready. Jamila takes a step back and looks at her work with approval.

Daisy is stunning. Between her eyes, her dark raven hair, and her voluptuous figure, she could be a dead ringer for Elizabeth Taylor as Maggie in *Cat on a Hot Tin Roof*.

"Meela, I'm so scared. What if I forget the words? What if..." Daisy panics.

Jamila takes a tissue and dabs her tears.

"Shhh," Jamila quiets her. "You stop all that, Daisy. You've been rehearsing for weeks. You know that song inside and out."

Jamila gently turns Daisy's face and touches up her blush.

"Okay." Daisy lets out a deep breath.

Jamila gives her a warm smile. "Sit tight, baby girl."

Jamila heads to the bar and makes a beeline for Cleo, the Kitten Heel's head bartender and MC. She's chatting with patrons and wiping down the bar when Jamila approaches. Cleo's a full-figured Black woman with smooth chestnut brown skin who is never without makeup or her signature sleek, high ponytail. As always, her face is flawless and there isn't a hair out of place.

Cleo greets Jamila with a warm smile. "What's your poison, Jamila?"

"I'll take two shots of Jameson, Ms. Cleo."

Cleo throws the bottle in the air causing it to flip four times before catching it. She then pours each shot all while maintaining eye contact with Jamila, not spilling a drop. Jamila and the patrons all applaud. Cleo takes a bow and gives them a wink.

"Here you go, sweetness." Cleo hands her the shot glasses.

"One of these days you're going to teach me how to do that." Jamila smirks.

"Trade secret, Miss Thang." Cleo blows her a kiss.

Jamila blows her a kiss right back before making her way back to the dressing room. As usual, the Kitten Heel is packed, and the vibe is electric. Jamila waves and smiles at some of the regulars. Every employee from Ms. Liz, the cabaret owner, to the performers—whom she affectionately calls 'the kittens'—work hard to not only put on a fun and entertaining show, they also put a lot of effort into giving the cabaret a playful and welcoming atmosphere. This has played a big part in why the Kitten Heel has thrived for thirty-plus years.

When Jamila returns, she hands Daisy the whiskey before downing a shot herself. Instead of drinking, Daisy holds the shot glass so tightly Jamila thinks she might break it. Carefully taking it out of her hand, Jamila puts it down and takes Daisy's hands in hers.

"Watch me," Jamila says softly.

She takes a deep breath in through her nose and slowly blows it out of her mouth.

"Now you. Slowly breathe in and slowly breathe out."

Jamila watches Daisy mimic her and smiles, remembering her first time on the main stage. She was a nervous wreck. Sweaty palms and dizzy spells almost stopped her from performing, but more troubling was the doubt. Thinking that she made a mistake moving to LA, that she wasn't good enough, and that the crowd would hate her. Those thoughts had consumed her so strongly that Ms. Liz had to calm her down. If it weren't for her and some of the more seasoned kittens offering their love and support, Jamila doesn't know where she would be now.

The Kitten Heel is Jamila's home away from home and has been for the past three years. And while working as a performer and cocktail waitress has been a fun experience, it isn't Jamila's dream. Ms. Liz understands this. She knows her employees are all aspiring to become big names in the entertainment industry, so she offers a flexible schedule. It's especially helpful when a pilot season or a commercial audition comes up. It's not unheard of for the kittens to help each other out by taking on an extra shift to cover for somebody. This has been Jamila's life since she left her sleepy little town of Harrisburg, Nebraska, and got on a Greyhound bus to make her dreams of stardom come true. A good portion of her days is spent rehearsing, going to auditions, or waitressing and/or performing at the Kitten Heel.

"Do you feel better?" Jamila asks.

"Yeah, I do. Thanks." Daisy grins.

"That's what I want to hear. Now close your eyes and let's finish making you more ravishing," Jamila says.

Daisy does as she's told while Jamila applies fake wispy lashes finishing her look. When she's done Jamila turns Daisy toward the mirror.

"What do you think?" Jamila beams as she waits for Daisy's reaction.

"I love it!" Daisy squeals.

"Good, now don't get too emotional. I don't have time to redo it," Jamila jokes. "Take the shot and relax. You're going to do great."

Daisy drinks the shot and shakes out her jitters. "Thanks again, Jamila! You're the best."

"No problem, sugar. You go out there and make them pant," Jamila giggles.

Daisy takes another deep breath and gives Jamila

an apprehensive smile before heading backstage. Cleo takes the stage.

"Hello kids, and welcome to the Kitten Heel Cabaret." The audience applauds and cheers. "I see some familiar faces in the crowd. Welcome back, and for our newcomers, you're in for a special treat. Making her debut on the main stage, our little sex pot herself, Miss Daisy!"

Daisy looks at Jamila, who gives her a smile and a thumbs-up. Daisy nods and goes on stage. She goes into a sultry rendition of "Zou Bisou Bisou," and the audience is eating out the palm of her hand. She sways her hips, blows kisses, and sits on a couple of laps. Jamila claps as she watches her; the girl's a natural.

Charmaine, another kitten and Jamila's friend, stands by her and watches with a huge grin on her face. Soon the two are dancing and singing along with Daisy. That's one of the many reasons Jamila loves working here. The rat race and constant audition rejections are mentally exhausting, but the minute she sets foot in the Kitten Heel, all those anxious feelings go away. Everyone here roots for each other. No one vies for more stage time or bitches about not getting enough tips. When one of them succeeds, they all do.

When Daisy finishes her set, she gets a rousing round of applause followed by roses and cash littering the stage. Ms. Liz had the ingenious idea of having several bouquets of roses available for purchase when folks first enter the cabaret so they can throw them at their favorite performers.

Jamila hugs Daisy the second she gets off stage.

"Jamila, they loved me!" Daisy cries, tears of joy streaming down her glittered cheeks.

"Of course, they did." Jamila wipes Daisy's tears.

"You did such a great job out there, babe," Charmaine says, hugging Daisy.

"Thank you, Char."

The three women celebrate Daisy's stage debut with glasses of champagne, more hugs, and a lot of laughter. After the cabaret closes at three in the morning, Jamila gives them a lift home. She made sure not to drink too much so she could be the designated driver. The last thing she wants is for her friends to take a ride share at this time of night.

The Whiskey Barrel, the bar next to the Kitten Heel, is still going strong. A group of loud and drunk women just went in, one of them wearing a tiara and sash that reads, "Bride-to-Be." The Whiskey Barrel's owner, Ray, is a great guy, but he and his security don't always use discretion when it comes to whom they let in. There have been more than a few times where businessmen, politicians, and overall rich assholes made their way from the bar to the Kitten Heel trying to solicit the girls for less than appealing services. Ms. Liz doesn't suffer fools and gladly makes them aware that their presence is no longer welcome at her establishment.

Case in point, Jamila sees Tennille being harassed by a man old enough to be her dad. Tennille and her friends often come to the Kitten Heel during Karaoke Fridays and have become favorite patrons of Jamila and the other girls.

"Wait, girls," Jamila says getting Daisy's and Charmaine's attention.

They notice Tennille on her phone trying to ignore the man who is getting uncomfortably close to her. Clearly scared, Tennille avoids looking at him. Without a second thought, Jamila runs up to her and hugs her.

"T! Girl, where have you been? We were waiting for you all night at the cabaret. You missed one hell of a show," Jamila laughs.

"Oh, hi, Meela. I'm so glad to see you. I thought you'd be gone by now."

"No, me, Daisy, and Char are getting ready to bounce. Let me give you a ride home."

"Thank you." Jamila watches as what looks like relief spreads across Tennille's face.

Jamila leads Tennille away, talking her ear off about Daisy's performance. The man grabs Jamila's arm.

"Maybe you and your friends can give me an encore. And maybe this one can join you," he slurs. The man is white, but his skin looks reddish. His hair is thinning, and he looks like a hot mess in his ill-fitting, light gray suit that's a size too big and ugly as sin.

"No, thank you. Please let go of my arm," Jamila says calmly.

Ramone, the security guard from the cabaret, comes over. He always stays behind until every girl has left. He's six foot, eight inches of solid muscle with slicked black hair, tanned skin, and tattoos covering both arms. As a former football player and marine, he's scary as hell but a total sweetheart to the girls.

"Is there a problem here?" Ramone barks.

"No, no problem." The drunk man looks like he's about to piss himself.

Ramone walks the ladies to Jamila's car.

"You ladies get home safe okay," Ramone says.

"We will. Thanks, Ramone."

"My pleasure," he smiles.

As Jamila drives out of the parking lot, she can tell Tennille is still a little shaken up.

"T, sweetie," Jamila says gently, "why were you outside a bar by yourself at three in the morning? I know you didn't go out there alone."

Tennille looks up at her, a forlorn look on her pretty face. "Morgan ditched me to hook up with some guy. We used our fake IDs to get in."

Jamila smirks. "That certainly takes me back." Charmaine and Daisy nod and laugh in agreement. "Well, babe, I certainly hope you learned your lesson."

"I did. No more fake IDs, Kitten Heel only, and no Morgan."

"Good, now let's get you home." Jamila smiles at her.

"Thank you."

"Anytime," Jamila winks.

Tennille gives Jamila a warm smile and starts to look more relaxed.

Hours later, Jamila quietly enters the apartment so she doesn't wake her boyfriend, Barry.

She dances into the living room humming "Zou Bisou Bisou," when she hears a faint giggle. A faint female giggle, followed by moans.

Jamila slowly walks to the bedroom door, her heart thumping like she's in a horror movie. Maybe if she walks slowly enough, it will further delay the inevitable betrayal. When she pushes it open, she finds Barry serving back shots to some bitch with a pixie cut. Both are butt naked and his little friend is throwing her ass back hard.

"Barry, baby. I'm about to come," the chick moans.

"Come on this dick, baby. You're so wet. My God!" Barry smacks her ass.

Jamila can't find her voice for a second. She and Barry have been together for six years. He followed her to L.A. from Nebraska to pursue a screenwriting career. He also wanted to make sure she was safe and taken care of, but it didn't take long for the stereotypical L.A. lifestyle to get to him. He went out of his way to get rid of his accent and started hanging out with the dipshit, small dick assholes from the literary agency he works at. Soon after, he started putting down Jamila's dream when she wasn't booking enough jobs.

"Don't you think you should consider that this isn't the right path for you?" Barry had suggested.

They were having breakfast one morning and Jamila had just told him she didn't book a job. She was already feeling raw and hopeless, and instead of offering her salve, he poured salt into the wound.

"Barry, what are you saying?" Jamila asked, her eyes tearing up.

"I'm not trying to hurt you, but this acting thing isn't working for you. Maybe you should give something else a try."

Give something else a try? He'd said that as if acting was her hobby, not a career goal.

If his complete lack of faith in her weren't enough, he's also tried on more than one occasion to get her to quit the cabaret. His reason was he felt embarrassed that she worked there. They eventually sat down and had a long talk, agreeing to get on the same page. But clearly, Jamila was the only one actually trying.

"Barry?" Jamila speaks softly.

Barry jumps and turns around, covering his dick and trying to shield his little plaything like Jamila can't see her.

"Jamila...um...I didn't want you to find out this way."

"Find out what, Barry?"

Barry takes his "friend's" hand and pulls her to his side, wrapping his arm around her waist while she has a sheet wrapped around her. "You remember, Carise, right? She's the receptionist at my office."

"Barry, I don't give a fuck what she does for a living! I want to know why you were balls deep in her."

Carise puts on a robe and heads for the door. "You two should talk. I'll be in the living room."

"Is that my fucking robe?" Jamila notices.

Carise gives Jamila a wide-eyed look before turning to Barry unsure of what to do.

"Jamila, is that really important right now?" He asks.

"She took my man; she's not taking my clothes!"

Carise takes off the robe and puts on one of Barry's t-shirts before leaving.

Jamila and Barry stare at each other. Him with discomfort and guilt, and her with anger and sadness.

"Look, Jamila. I haven't been invested in our relationship for a while. You work at that place, your unrealistic dream to be an actress—"

"How the hell is my dream any less realistic than yours?"

"Because we're in two different places in our lives. My boss promised me that he was going to read my script. Do you know how huge that is? I'm moving up in the industry and you're not."

Is he fucking serious?

"My last residual check helped us with our bills last month, and I'm going to start my five-episode appearance in *Harbor Medical* in a few weeks."

"And then what, Meela? Where's your next job?"

"That's what auditions are for asshole. And it's not like I don't make decent tips at the Kitten Heel."

"That's another thing. You were only supposed to be working there a year; it's been three."

"So?"

"Meela, how do you think it makes me feel having to tell people you work there? You're naked on stage having drunk assholes throw money at you. It's embarrassing."

Jamila couldn't believe what she was hearing. The Kitten Heel isn't a strip club and even if it was, who cares? Jamila felt at home there, and it's helped to support them. Yes, Barry makes more money but that didn't give him the right to belittle her.

"I'm asking you to leave," Barry continues. "Carise is going to move in. She's on her way to becoming an agent and it just makes sense for she and I to be together."

"Where am I supposed to go?"

"Can't you stay with what's her name from the club?"

"Cabaret, Barry! It's a fucking cabaret! And her name is Charmaine."

"Whatever. Can't you stay with her?"

"She already has three roommates. Char wouldn't have room for me."

"Okay, well. I'll put you up in a hotel for a few days until you can find something. I feel bad so..."

"You feel bad? Barry, the statement 'I feel bad' is for when you sideswipe a parked car, not for when you implode someone's life. Especially when you're supposed to love that person."

"I do love you, Jamila. I just don't want to be with you anymore."

Jamila rushes over to the closet grabbing an overnight bag and anything within her reach. The truly fucked up part about all of this is, except for some clothes and a few toiletries, Jamila really doesn't have much in terms of belongings.

When she's done packing all her stuff she heads for the door.

"Jamila, wait."

She turns around and faces Barry. "What?"

He gets up and puts on his boxers. After retrieving his wallet, he takes out some cash and offers it to her. Jamila looks down at the money and then up at him before punching him in the dick.

"Fuck! Damnit, Jamila!"

"Fuck you, Barry," She says walking out the door. She's unsure of what to do next, but it won't include Barry.

2

AMARI

Amari walks into the Echo office building like a king surveying his palace. Each person he walks by warmly greets him. Being the youngest VP of Original Programming for Echo, the world's biggest streaming service, is a dream come true. He's worked damn hard to get to this position.

He walks by a group of ladies sitting in the building's lobby. They all smile, and a couple wave. Amari politely smiles and waves back. Amari gets his fair share of attention from women. Being six-foot-two with a body sculpted by heavy-weight training helps and having amazing genetics doesn't hurt. Even though he is the picture-perfect man, he tends to keep women looking for a relationship at arm's length. He does dabble in a one-night stand once or twice a week, but he's not interested in getting into anything serious again. He's made it a habit not to get mixed up in anything that could lead to a relationship.

Amari boards the elevator and is greeted by the operator. "Good morning, Mr. Hawkins."

"Good morning, George. How's Judy?" Amari replies.

"Nagging me about that damn cruise."

"Man, you better take that woman on a vacation, as many years as she's put up with you," Amari grins.

"Yeah, yeah. I will. Figured I'd surprise her for our anniversary."

"That's what's up."

"Forty-first floor. You have a good one, Mr. Hawkins."

"You too, George. Let me know how the surprise turns out."

"Will do."

Ever since Amari was a kid, his teachers would fuck up his name, so he's made it his mission to memorize the names of a majority of the people he's encountered. He believes that knowing a person's moniker is an important step in knowing who they are as an individual. This became especially important considering his leadership role. The folks at

Echo who are considered "lower rung" employees love him. It was his goal for them to know there is someone in one of the big corner offices who will go to bat for them.

It was Amari who helped negotiate the janitors getting their raises when they threatened to go on strike. He's always been the type to look out for the underdog.

The minute he gets off the elevator, Amari is joined by his assistant, Bree, who is waiting for him with a cup of coffee.

"Morning, Bree."

"Morning, Mr. Hawkins." She hands him the cup. "Your ten o'clock has been rescheduled to Tuesday at two, your meeting with Mr. Nunez is in an hour, and Ms. Roman called...again."

"Just keep telling her I'm not in."

"Got it! Your sister, mother, and niece will see you for lunch at twelve-thirty. And my mom wanted me to thank you again for the ballet tickets. Seeing Kima Terrell perform has been on her bucket list."

"It was no problem; Ms. Terrell is a good friend. I'm glad your mom had a great time. Speaking of moms, were you able to make the reservations?"

"I did but when I called your mother to remind her, she..."

"Made you cancel the reservations and insisted on me coming to the house for lunch."

"Yeah." Bree smiles sheepishly. "She said something about you not spending money all…"

"Willy nilly." Amari playfully rolls his eyes. "It's okay, Bree. She's formidable. You really didn't stand a chance, but I had to try."

"It was nice to see where you get it from."

Amari chuckles at her comment. "Trust, I am a kitten compared to that woman."

"That I wholeheartedly believe. Mr. Dawson is waiting in your office."

"Thank you."

When Amari enters his office he finds his co-worker, frat brother, and best friend sitting at his desk.

"Nigga, is there a reason you're in my chair?" he says, closing the door.

Keith gets up and takes a seat in front of the desk. "Just wanted to see how it feels to be the HNIC."

Amari shakes his head and claims his seat. Keith Dawson has been Amari's ace boon since grad school when they bonded over pledging the same frat, Alpha Phi Alpha. So it's no coincidence they ended up at the same company. Keith is the

Associate VP of Unscripted Programming at Echo. Amari helped poach Keith from Netflix.

"You already are the HNIC," Amari remarks.

"Yes, but you are *thee* HNIC. It's only a matter of time before they add that 'senior' to your title, bruh."

"Really? What you heard?"

"Nigga, please. With the high ass ratings that *Sisterhood* is getting, they'd be crazy not to promote you."

"Thanks, man."

"Now on to more important stuff. How did last night go with that fine ass sista from the club?"

"It was cool. We had some dranks, talked a bit, then I took her to my place."

"And?"

"And, nigga, what you think?"

"No, I know y'all fucked. I mean do you see a future with this one?"

Here we go.

Amari lets out a sigh.

Ever since Keith got his act together and married his long-time love, Erika, he thinks Amari needs to get back out there and take the plunge. The problem is, the last time Amari took the plunge was with Layla, and that relationship came with more baggage than LAX, Dulles International, and JFK combined. For now, he's good with being alone and having no attachments. He just wishes his friends and family could get with the program.

"No, no future. Just…"

"Fun. Yeah, I know but c'mon Mar, eventually that shit is going to get old. And you ain't getting any younger."

"Motherfucker, I'm only thirty-three."

"You say that now but soon it'll be 'I'm only fifty-three' and you don't want to be the middle-aged nigga scouting for pussy in the club."

"I promise it won't come to that." Amari lets out a deep breath. "Bree told me Layla called again. She must have figured out I changed my cell number, so she keeps calling here."

"What the fuck does she want? And why are you just now telling me?"

"The answer to both questions is I don't know. I don't want to find out what she wants, and I guess I figured if I ignored her long enough, she'd stop."

"How long has she been calling?"

"About three weeks."

"You might have to bite the bullet and talk to her."

"Naw, fuck that. I don't want anything to do with her manipulative ass."

"I get it but for real, Mar. Don't let what that bitch did to you sour you on finding something real."

"Duly noted. And I appreciate your concern. Now kindly get the fuck out my office," Amari chuckles.

Keith laughs. "Aight. Erika wants to know when you'll be joining us for dinner?"

"As soon as she stops trying to set me up with the chicks at her salon."

Erika owns a beauty shop and has tried to set Amari up with everyone. From her clients to her staff and their sisters, cousins, and aunties.

"I'll let her know."

"Thanks."

At noon, Amari heads to his mother's house. Since he's running late, he sends her a text letting her know. Being the only male in his family is a mixed bag. Granted, he understands women a lot better than most dudes but it usually comes at the expense of him fucking up beforehand. Amari's the youngest of four children. He has three sisters—Kenya, Iman, and Zuri—who are all very protective of him even though they are scattered across the world. Zuri lives in Kansas City with her wife Joann where they own an antique store. Iman lives in London with her husband Sam, and their daughter Chloe. Iman works as the managing director for the London Opera Company. And Kenya lives here in L.A. with their mom, Vonetta, along with her twenty-year-old daughter, Tennille. Kenya works at LAX as a TSA supervisor. After her divorce six years ago, Kenya moved from Chicago wanting to be near their mother, and she's lived here ever since. Her daughter Tennille attends UCLA where she's studying film history.

Amari has her set up with an internship at Echo this summer. She's the niece he's closest to, mainly because he hasn't seen Chloe in person since she was two years old and she's four now.

Amari drums his hands on the steering wheel, buzzing with excitement. He can't wait to share his big news with his family. His meeting with Mr. Nunez, Echo's CFO, was amazing. They are looking to diversify their current lineup of original films because it was starting to look as white as every Oscar night––the main reason Amari was called in was to fix their original programming. Every show or film his successor, Harvey, a white dude championed failed to gain an audience with the Black community. Black folks are one of Echo's largest demographics and the shows Harvey got greenlit were all subjected to the wrath of Black Twitter.

Amari went over Harvey's head and pitched the CEO a show he found in the slush pile. The show is called *Sisterhood*. It's about four Black sorority sisters at a fictional HBCU. Their story unfolds over the course of forty years as the viewers follow them from their sophomore year until they're in their sixties. It's currently Echo's most talked about show having garnered thirteen million views for its premiere; the numbers just keep going up. It was recently picked up for three more seasons.

The success led to Harvey quietly being transferred to another department while Amari took his job. All this eventually resulted in Mr. Nunez approving the budget for six more new shows and five films. Amari is putting his stamp on the streaming world and making big moves. His goal of being named Executive Vice President of Original Programming by the time he's forty is just within his reach.

No Black man has ever achieved a leadership role that big in streaming and he wants to be the first.

As for the whole Layla thing, he's keeping mum about that. Shit, telling Keith was enough. His mom, who always liked Layla, will probably try to convince him to get back with her and there is no way that's happening, not after what she did.

Whipping his Bentley into a parking space, Amari parks his car and jumps out. Mrs. Gordon is watering her lawn per usual. She's lived next door to his family for decades., and though she's in her sixties, Mrs. Gordon looks forty-something. Her salt and pepper hair is pulled back in a ponytail and her tawny skin only has a few wrinkles. She's in her usual loungewear of a collegiate t-shirt—courtesy of a grandchild, no doubt––and yoga pants.

"Hello, Mrs. Gordon," Amari belts out, waving his hand high in the air.

"Hey, baby. How are you?"

"Doing well, ma'am."

"You know, my granddaughter is in town from Atlanta—"

"I'm sorry, Mrs. Gordon but Mom is waiting for me. Give your granddaughter's info to her when you get a chance."

"Will do!"

Before Mrs. Gordon can add anything else, Amari rushes into the house.

This is getting ridiculous.

It's like he has a sign hanging from his neck that says, "Desperately single, please help!" Ever since he and Layla broke up, Erika, his mom, and sisters, hell even his mail carrier, have tried to introduce him to somebody. And honestly, he's tired of having to repeatedly tell people that he doesn't want a relationship right now. Or maybe ever.

It's not like Amari doesn't get it. When he was with Layla and they were happy, things were great. So, he appreciates the people in his life wanting that for him again. But do they have to bring it up *every time* they see him?

"Hey hey!" he calls out.

"We're out here, Pooh Bear," Vonetta calls out.

I'll be eighty years old and she'll be over a hundred still calling me that.

Amari shakes his head and smiles. She never gets tired of using his childhood nickname. When Amari was four years old, he was obsessed with Winnie the Pooh and his mom has been calling him Pooh Bear since. And even at his big age, he still finds it endearing.

When he gets to the backyard, he finds Vonetta, Kenya, and Tennille sitting at the patio table playing cards. They look like three generations of the same person. All three have light bronze skin, hazel eyes, and long straightened hair. The only difference is Tennille has dyed her hair a light brown-blondish color while his mom and sister have dark brown hair. Amari's hair is dark brown as well. It's currently styled in a drop-low fade that connects with his tapered beard. He and Zuri have the same skin tone, while Iman is darker than Kenya. Amari, Zuri, and Iman all also have dark brown eyes. The kids at school used to tease Kenya, implying she was adopted until they saw Vonetta.

"Hey Mom, Ken, Miss T." Amari hugs and kisses each one of them.

"Hey, Uncle Pooh," Tennille says, smiling.

Amari takes a seat while his mom deals him in.

"So, what was this exciting news you texted?" Vonetta asks.

"I am going to be adding six more shows and five original movies to Echo these next few quarters! I'm on my way, Mom, I can feel it."

"I'm happy for you, baby, but we all knew that was going to happen. As driven as you are, you'll be running Echo in no time."

"Thank you, Mommy," Amari says, kissing her cheek.

Vonetta smiles and squeezes his hand.

"What did you think I was going to tell you?" Amari asks.

"I thought you met a woman." Vonetta shrugs.

"Me too," Kenya agrees.

"So did I," Tennille adds.

Amari lets out a sigh and gets up. "Who wants some lemonade?"

All three ladies raise their hands. Amari heads into the kitchen. Vonetta has lived in this house ever since Amari was five. She even has some of the same stuff from back then. A clock radio—that miraculously still works—the same old cookie jar she got at a garage sale, and the cat clock, which doesn't work but she keeps it for sentimental value.

Amari is always teasing her about being a pack rat, but he loves seeing these old things too. It reminds him of simpler times. Amari once offered to buy his mom a new home closer to him in Culver City, but she said Inglewood is close enough. She did take him up on his offer to upgrade her appliances.

A pot of Cajun beef stew simmers on the stove. The smell takes him back to his childhood. His mouth waters as he anticipates that first taste. No matter how many times Amari has his mom's famous dishes, it's always like having them for the first time. He tries to sneak a taste, but Tennille catches him.

"What you doin', Uncle Pooh?"

"Mind your business, Miss T." Amari blows on

the spoon and tastes the stew. "I know one thing, if I do get a woman soon, she better be able to cook like this. I can't be the only one throwing down in the kitchen."

Tennille laughs and takes his spoon so she can sneak a taste too.

"What else do you want in a woman, Uncle Pooh?"

"Why? You want to hook me up with one of your professors?" Amari mocks.

"No, seriously. You're constantly telling us that you'd rather be alone than in a drama-filled relationship, but you've never actually said the type of relationship you want."

Amari steps back astonished at how much Tennille has actually paid attention. "The type that includes a woman who is thicker than London fog and fine as hell." Tennille rolls her eyes. "What?" Amari grins.

"C'mon, be for real."

Amari's eyebrows scrunch together. "I think I just want someone to look out for me. Someone who will take care of me. Don't get me wrong, I'm a grown-ass man, but I look out for a lot of people. And I don't mind because it's in my nature to take care of folks.

But it would be nice to have someone who did the same for me."

"That sounds reasonable."

"Yeah, well, I don't know about that. She may not be out there."

"She is."

Amari smiles at his niece's optimism. "How's Morgan? You two still getting into trouble." He smirks.

"Morgan and I are done-zo. We aren't friends anymore."

"What? Why? Ya'll have been tight for a while."

"Yeah, well, we became un-tight when she ditched me for some dude at a..." Tennille stops herself. She turns away to finish pouring the lemonade for Kenya and Vonetta.

"At a what, Tennille?" Amari frowns.

Amari is the cool uncle, but he will always put his foot down if he thinks Tennille is doing something that could get her hurt.

"At a bar. We were supposed to be having a girl's night but when we got there, she ditched me, and I ended up getting a ride with Jamila," Tennille whispers.

"The chick from the karaoke place?"

"It's not a karaoke place. It's a cabaret that hosts karaoke once a week, but yes."

"You're only twenty. How did you even get into a bar?"

Tennille looks away, and Amari can see she's embarrassed by how her night unfolded. He can't really hold it against her. He did plenty of dumb shit when he was her age. Plus, Kenya is overbearing. Tennille stayed at home instead of moving into the dorms at Kenya's urging. Amari tried to convince Kenya to let Tennille live on campus, but she wouldn't budge. Tennille needing a break from her mom isn't unbelievable.

"With a fake ID."

Amari clenched his jaw. "You know better than to do something like that."

"I know."

"I'm not going to tell on you but promise me you won't do something like that again."

"I promise. After what happened with Morgan, there's no way."

"Were you safe?"

"Yeah, nothing happened, Uncle Pooh. Just some drunk guy trying to talk to me."

Amari can tell she's downplaying the encounter for his benefit.

"What did that motherfucker look like?"

Tennille shrugs. "Like a balding, middle-aged white dude."

"Middle-aged!"

"Uncle Pooh, keep your voice down."

"Sorry," he whispers," but if I find out what that piece of shit looks like, I'ma fuck him up."

"Don't worry. Ramone, he's the security guy at the Kitten Heel, he scared the hell out of the drunk dude."

"Good. I'm glad he and your friend were there to help you." Amari puts his arm around her. "And you were right to get rid of Morgan. She shouldn't have left you hanging like that."

"Thank you." Tennille sips her lemonade. "I want to repay Jamila. She not only got me home, but she sent me a text the next day to make sure I was okay."

"That was kind of her."

"Yeah, it was. I think I'll buy her coffee or something."

"Or you can take her to lunch."

"That could work."

"I swear that lady will talk your damn ear off if you let her," Vonetta says fanning herself as she comes in the backdoor.

Amari smiles. "Mrs. Gordon?"

"Yes. Just blabbing away about one of her granddaughters over the fence."

"She must be done watering her lawn."

"Yep, now she's watering her flower bed and decided to chat with me and your sist—" Vonetta stops talking and looks at Amari and Tennille suspiciously.

Vonetta marches up to Amari with a commanding and unflinching presence.

"Bend down and let me smell your breath, Amari."

Amari. Not Pooh Bear. *Shit!* Amari bends down close enough for Vonetta to get a good whiff.

"Hmmm," Vonetta says. She turns to her granddaughter. "Your turn little girl."

Tennille lets her smell her breath. Vonetta backs away and looks at them with playful disappointment.

"Ya'll know to wait until I say it's ready. That stew still got a few minutes left. Don't you touch it again, you hear?"

"Yes, ma'am," Amari and Tennille both reply.

3

JAMILA

*J*amila gets up and stretches. "Ow! Fuck."

All she's done is slightly turn her head, but it's caused a throbbing pain to radiate from the base of her neck to the back of her head. She's been sleeping on Charmaine's lumpy ass sofa for the past two days. At this point, something has got to give. Between the aches and pains, and Charmaine's creepy cat staring at her all the time, Jamila is ready to lose her shit.

Maybe I should have taken Barry's money. Shit, I've officially gone off the deep end.

Her phone buzzes, and it's a text from Tennille.

> Hey, I wanted to thank you for the other night. Do you want to meet up for lunch?

> Sure. What time?

> How's 1 at the Lighthouse café? You know it?

Does she know it? Shit, Jamila practically lived at that place when she and Barry first moved out to L.A. Their comfort food is crazy delicious and you can't beat the price.

> Yeah, I do. See you at 1.

Jamila puts her phone down. *Today may not actually be so bad.*

Suddenly, she's interrupted by Fluffer Nutter. Jamila still can't believe Charmaine named her cat such a goofy ass name, especially when Demon would have been much better. It hops onto the coffee table and stares at Jamila like it's plotting to murder her.

It'll be a miracle if Jamila makes it on time, considering she has to wait until Charmaine and her roommates are done getting ready before she can get into the bathroom. After a frigid shower, trying to do something with her hair and digging through her duffle bag for acceptable attire, she eventually settles on her dance rehearsal outfit— black yoga pants, a white t-shirt with the Kitten Heel logo on the front, and a pair of comfy sneakers. The t-shirt is tied into a knot that stops under her breasts, and considering the Lighthouse is a popular spot for college students, Jamila's casual look won't make her stand out. It's a quarter past twelve by the time she manages to make it out of the house.

Jamila arrives at one on the dot, the Lighthouse is in the midst of the lunch rush. There are lots of college kids milling about and stuffing their faces before their next class. Jamila loves coming here because it reminds her of Archie's, the coffee shop she and her friends used to go to after school. There wasn't a lot going on in Harrisburg, so the kids would go to Archie's to grab a burger and just hang out.

Jamila searches for Tennille and finds her bright happy face sitting in a corner booth. It's a relief to see her smiling and she seems to be okay.

"Hi," Jamila smiles and hugs Tennille. "How are you?"

"I'm good. How are you? You look tired. Been rehearsing a lot, I bet."

"Not any more than usual. My haggard look is thanks to lack of sleep on the world's lumpiest couch and a cat that I'm starting to believe might be a demon."

"I'm sorry?" Tennille says looking confused.

Jamila tells her the whole story. When she's done Tennille takes her hand and squeezes it. "I'm so sorry, Jamila. Your ex is a major asshole."

"Thank you."

Tennille's eyes light up. "I know a place you can stay."

"Where?"

Instead of responding Tennille pulls out her phone and sends a flurry of text messages. Her phone buzzes and she sends off some more. This goes on for three minutes before she finally looks up and addresses Jamila.

"Okay, you're all set."

"All set for what?"

"To stay at my uncle's place."

"Um, no offense but...hell no."

"Why not?"

"I don't know him."

"Yeah, but you know me. C'mon Meela I wouldn't

offer to place you somewhere dangerous. My uncle is a nice guy. He's smart, funny, handsome—"

Jamila lets out an exasperated sigh and pinches the bridge of her nose.

"Tennille, I am not interested in being set up with someone or living with a stranger."

"I know, and I get it, but he's so great. He is not creepy or weird at all. I swear."

"If you're able to offer me a place to stay then why can't it be your grandma's house?"

"You've heard me talk about my mom, she's just like my grams, which means she can be a lot. Besides my uncle will give you space and privacy. That's a guarantee. I can't say the same about my mom or grams."

"And he's okay with this?"

"Yeah, he's heard me mention you tons of times, and he knows how you helped me out."

Jamila is still not convinced. The idea of living with some rando, no matter how much Tennille talks him up, isn't something she's interested in. She'd rather take her chances with Fluffer Nutter.

"It's a nice place; I stay there sometimes. He has three guest rooms, a state-of-the-art kitchen, and a full bathroom in each bedroom. And let me tell you that shower is...there are no words."

"No," Jamila says.

"Meela!" Tennille whines.

"What? Girl, do you not hear yourself? What you're proposing is batshit."

"Why? Are you scared we're going to sell you into human trafficking?"

"Now I am."

"Meela, please. Please let me do this for you."

"T..." Jamila sighs.

"Can I at least show you the place before you turn it down?"

Jamila looks at her suspiciously. "Why are you so invested in me moving in with your uncle?"

"Honestly, because I'm worried about him. He's been acting like he's fine, but I know he's lonely. You need a place to stay and he could use the company."

"He has a family, and I'm assuming, friends."

"He does but no one can rely solely on their family for companionship and his friends are all married. He's the only holdout."

"Fine. I will come look at it for ten minutes..."

"Twenty."

"Fifteen, then I'm out."

"Great!"

"I better not get murdered."

"Girl, chill. You won't."

They arrive at the house thirty minutes later. Jamila drops her gym bag near the door and looks around. *Tennille wasn't lying, this place is amazing.*

"Let me show you around!" Tennille says excitedly. "The house has an open living room, kitchen, and dining areas. Four bedrooms, two bathrooms, all upstairs, and a small office downstairs."

"You sound like a real estate listing," Jamila says unimpressed.

"Hush. I'm getting to the good part."

Jamila and Tennille walk onto the large balcony.

"A grassy backyard! You can have the kittens come by to rehearse. There's also a covered patio and large deck, and the pièce de résistance—a built-in BBQ and a hot tub."

"Why is that the pièce de résistance?"

"Hello? Hot tub," Tennille says stating the obvious.

The two make their way back to the living room.

"Okay, so what do you think?" Tennille's voice is filled with excitement.

"It's nice. If I ever want to rob somebody, this will be the first place I hit."

With the way my luck is going lately, I may have to start doing that.

"Meela, c'mon. Be serious. This place is great and

so is my Uncle Pooh." Tennille gives her a big bright smile.

Tennille is a sweet girl but she's still a kid. Only three years out of high school. She clearly thought that merely showing Jamila the house would clinch the deal. She thinks that maybe between the house and her uncle, Jamila will be swept off her feet.

Not going to happen.

Jamila is twenty-six and knows that life is not a fairytale.

"It's nice but I'm still not living here. I gave you fifteen minutes, and now I'm out."

"Technically, it's only been twelve."

"What are you going to do? Make me stand here for three more minutes?"

The front door opens, and an older woman walks in. She looks to be in her fifties with a faint crow's feet etched into her tawny skin. She has on light gray sweatpants and a white t-shirt, and her graying wavy hair is pulled back into a ponytail.

"Hello," she greets them.

"Hi," Jamila and Tennille respond in unison.

"Yolanda, I want you to meet my friend, Jamila. Jamila, Yolanda is my uncle's housekeeper." Tennille smiles.

"Oh! A pleasure to meet you." Jamila shakes her hand.

"Likewise," Yolanda grins. "Tennille, does your uncle know you're here?"

"Kind of."

Yolanda rolls her eyes. "Well, you better *kind of* make yourself scarce. He's on his way home and you know how he feels about people dropping by unannounced."

"He gets off at five, it's only three," Tennille says.

"He had an appointment this afternoon, so he ducked out early."

Yolanda goes to the kitchen and grabs some cleaning supplies before heading upstairs.

Hearing that Tennille's uncle will be home soon is all Jamila needed to hear. Knowing that the owner of the house will be walking in at any minute, Jamila is definitely getting the fuck out of dodge, especially since she was already set to leave.

As if she was reading her thoughts Tennille gives her a reassuring smile. "Don't worry, I'm his favorite niece. He won't mind us being here."

"Does not fucking matter." Jamila takes her car keys out of her purse and heads to the door.

But before she can make her way out, the door opens, and in comes a man so fine she forgets all sense of space and time. He's fit, thick, and hand-some with full lips surrounded by a shortly trimmed beard, strong Black features, and the body of a god. He has on tan pants, a white linen shirt, and a light brown sweater. He looks like a tall, sexy Carlton.

"Hello?" he says, looking right at Jamila.

"Hello," she chokes out.

His voice. It's husky. Manly. Powerful.

I have to get the fuck out of this house.

"I...I was just leaving," Jamila sputters.

"Okay," he replies.

Jamila's brain is telling her to leave but her legs aren't cooperating. Her feet remain firmly planted as he stares back at her. She gazes at him, memorizing every feature like she'll never see him again.

"Uncle Pooh, this is my friend Jamila. Jamila this is my uncle, Amari."

He turns his attention to Tennille. "The same Jamila you asked me to let move in and I told you hell no?"

Jamila turns and gives Tennille a deadly look. "What happened to *your all set*?"

"All set. You told her she could live here? You told a *stranger* she can live here? T, this ain't your house. And I'm sorry but were you willing to move in here without even meeting me? I could be a serial killer. I'm not, but you didn't know that."

"No, I was not. I told Tennille that I didn't want to move in."

"Then why are you here?"

"Um..."

Shit! In hindsight, coming here was a huge mistake. What exactly could she tell him? *I came here because your niece wouldn't shut up until I at least saw your house.* That just sounds weird.

"You know what, it doesn't matter because I'm leaving. It was nice to meet you, you have a lovely home that, again, I do not want to live in. Just want to make that clear... Okay, I'm going to leave now."

"Are you sure this time?" Amari asks.

Jamila lets out an embarrassed chuckle and heads out the door. She gets in her car and takes her ass back to Charmaine's. Maybe if she asks really nicely, Barry will give her that hotel money after all.

4

AMARI

"Have you lost your damn mind? Where do you get off inviting some stranger into my house?"

"Uncle Pooh…"

"Don't you Uncle Pooh me. Answer my question."

"Okay, I shouldn't have done that, but did you see the way she was looking at you?"

"Like she was ready to spend the night and make him breakfast, lunch, and dinner," Yolanda says, coming down the stairs.

"How would you know? You were upstairs cleaning," Amari says.

"I was upstairs, but I was watching everything

happening down here. And that girl was practically drooling, and you know what? So, were you."

"I was not!" Amari argues.

"The hell." Yolanda rolls her eyes.

"Yes, you were," Tennille replies.

Yolanda and Tennille both respond at the same time.

"Look, I know everybody and their mother—including your own mother––has been on you about moving on after that heifer broke your heart, but it is time, Amari. I'm not saying let the girl move in but at least take her out for coffee or something," Yolanda suggests.

Amari wipes his hand over his face. He has way too many meddlers in his life.

"You see how I did that youngin'?" Yolanda says to Tennille, "I kept it simple. I didn't try to give him a roommate. Take notes. I'm going to get dinner prepped."

Amari turns his attention back to Tennille who is seemingly trying to smile her way out of trouble.

"Give me one good reason why I shouldn't call your mother and tell her about you being at that bar?"

"Because you said you wouldn't, and my actions may have been misguided but my heart was in the right place. Uncle Pooh, you can't convince me that you aren't lonely."

Amari lets out an annoyed breath. As much as he hates to admit it, he is a little lonely. Bringing women back to his place is fun during the act but when they leave, it's just him, and that's scary. The thing that scares him more though, is putting himself out there only to be hurt again.

"I get it, and I appreciate your concern, but do not pull some shit like that again."

"I won't. I swear."

"You heading out?"

"Um...Jamila was kind of my ride."

"So, you're staying for dinner and you're staying over?"

"If that's okay."

"Of course, it is."

"Thank you, Uncle Pooh."

The two hug and he rests his arm around her shoulder as they head to the kitchen to help Yolanda.

"I have to admit. You were definitely paying attention when I told you that I wanted a woman thick as London fog."

"Okay, ew. That's just sexist."

"You're the one trying to move her in. I thought you would be thrilled I noticed."

Later that night, Amari lies in his bed wrestling with the covers throughout the night. Tennille's words really stuck, and even worse, they weren't too far from the truth.

No matter how truthful she was, Tennille literally brought that girl into my house!

His mind wanders to Jamila. Holy shit, she was breathtaking! Her dark brown curly tresses in that messy bun plopped on the top of her head, and her curves were a sight to behold, and her face! It was nothing short of gorgeous. Her dreamy dark brown eyes against her golden-brown skin, heart-shaped lips, and cute little button nose made Amari's heart skip.

She's the type of woman who could stop traffic and probably could make any man bend to her will without even trying. Would it be so bad to take her out for coffee? He could make it an apology for being so brusque with her. But why did she come if she turned down T's offer? Whatever the reason, Amari wasn't disappointed in what he saw.

Don't go there, Mar. Layla seemed perfect, too.

Amari reaches over and grabs his cell phone

from the nightstand. He dials his work number and finds the deleted message Layla left today.

"Hello, Amari. How are you? I hope you're doing well. I don't know if your assistant has given you my messages. I suppose she has but you just aren't taking them. I get it. I do, but I really do need to speak with you. It's important. Please call me back. My number is still the same."

Call her back and talk about what? Her betrayal? How much of a fool did she make him out to be? Fuck her. Tennille is right, he is lonely. But he will not let being lonely make him lose his dignity. Not again.

IT'S BEEN TWO MONTHS, AND WHILE AMARI HAS BEEN busy with work and avoiding Layla, he can't get Jamila out of his head. It doesn't help that he saw her on TV not long after meeting her. She was on his favorite medical drama where she played a patient. The makeup people tried their best to make her look tired and haggard, but she still looked fine as hell. He's since peeped her IMDB page, checking out a few shows and made-for-TV movies she's been in, and Amari's impressed.

He keeps telling himself that it's strictly for work. Being on the pulse of all the new up-and-coming actors is part of the job. But deep down Amari knows he's full of shit. Jamila isn't just talented and beautiful, she's special. Her strength and vulnerability shine through in each performance and her allure is unmatched. Amari has met plenty of actresses and none of them have intrigued him the way Jamila has.

He desperately wants to see her again. Amari considered getting her number from Tennille but that would just open a can of worms in the form of Tennille, his mother, and sister asking twenty questions. Then because none of them can hold water, Zuri and Iman would be joining the interrogation soon after.

After a long day, Amari arrives home, looking forward to a nice long shower and vegging in front of the TV. The day was filled with one meeting after another. His team pitched three shows and all but one got shot down. They're currently busy courting LaWanda King––a New York Times bestselling author––whose best-selling novel, *Just an Ordinary Girl* is creating a feeding frenzy. Every streaming service is in a bidding war to get the rights. The main character, Kandia, is the role of a lifetime, and Black actresses from L.A. to the UK will be vying for that role. Then he had to attend meetings with the creative team for a ground-breaking show called *Sioux*, which will feature an all-indigenous cast and crew. And then there's the film project *Landslide*.

Its purpose is to aid as a comeback vehicle for Greta Chambers, the one-time child star who had several stints in rehab and is considered persona non grata in the industry. Echo's taking a big chance being the launch pad for her return to acting.

Amari's phone buzzes. It's Tennille.

"Hey T," Amari answers.

"It's Friday!" she cheers.

"Yeah, kiddo, I'm aware of that."

"The Kitten Heel has karaoke tonight. We haven't hung out in a while and you would get to see Jamila again." She sings the last part in a teasing tone.

"And what if I said I didn't want to see her again?" Amari mocks her tone.

"Then I'd know you're completely full of ... well, you know. Plus, saying you're exhausted after a long day would have been more believable."

"Can I use that excuse now?"

"No. Pick me up in an hour."

"Um... you can't tell me what to do, Miss. T."

"I can too. We all know you can't say no to me, Uncle Pooh. Besides, if you try to bail, I'll be forced to tell Ms. Gordon that you would love to go out with her granddaughter. And don't bother using my fake ID bar misadventure as a bargaining ploy. Because you and I both know that if you tell Mom, she'll be just as pissed at you for waiting so long to say something."

Fuck. She's right. The last thing Amari needs is to sit through a long-ass lecture from his sister followed by Ms. Gordon inviting him to lunch in the hopes of him hitting it off with her granddaughter—who he has already met. He bumped into her while visiting his mother and she talked his ear off about Atlanta. Apparently being long-winded is a genetic trait.

"Fine. I'll get you in an hour."

"Yay! This will be so much fun."

Amari is honestly excited to see Jamila again but there's no way in hell he's telling Tennille that.

Amari and Tennille enter the Kitten Heel. Its décor is giving him strong *Moulin Rouge* vibes. They definitely knocked it out of the park. The stage is red and heart-shaped, and it's like he stepped onto the set of the movie.

A pretty dark-haired woman who looks like 1950's Elizabeth Taylor's doppelganger approaches their table carrying a tablet.

"Hi, Tennille." She smiles.

"Hi, Daisy. This is my Uncle Amari."

"Pleased to meet you, handsome. Welcome to the Kitten Heel."

"Thank you. It's nice to meet you."

"What can I get you?"

"I'll have a beer, anything imported."

"Gotcha. And Tennille would you like your usual?"

"And what exactly is your usual?" Amari asks.

"Relax, Uncle Pooh. I always get a Shirley Temple."

"No worries, handsome. The Kitten Heel maybe eighteen and over, but we are very strict about carding."

"That's good to know. Thank you."

"Be back in a jiff."

Daisy heads over to the bar to get their drinks and comes back minutes later. Amari gives her a nice tip, and pleased at the gesture, she winks at him before sashaying away. The ladies here, without question, earn their pay. As Amari scans the cabaret, he notices all the kittens are in alluring negligees, corsets, and high heels.

"That cannot be comfortable. They on their feet serving drinks all night, and having to put up with all this unwanted attention by thirsty dudes ain't helping," Amari remarks.

"Uncle Pooh, they get tips from the way they dress. Trust, if anyone gets out-of-pocket these ladies can handle them," Tennille replies.

A rotund Black woman with a long silky ponytail enters the stage holding a microphone.

"Hello, and welcome to the Kitten Heel cabaret! I'm Cleo."

The audience cheers, some throwing roses at her feet.

"Aw, you all are too kind. Thank you, my darlings. Now as you regulars know it's the last Friday of the month."

"Oh, yeah. That's right!" Tennille says.

"What's going on?" Amari asks.

"Every last Friday of the month, all the girls do a special performance and there's no karaoke. That's why the place is packed."

Amari is relieved that karaoke is off the table. No doubt Tennille would have tried to make him do a duet.

"Coming to the stage, our sultry piece of sunshine from the cornhusker state, Ms. Jamila Washington as the grand dame, Ms. Josephine."

Amari is startled by how quickly the crowd

stands up and cheers. There are men throwing money and roses and Jamila hasn't even entered the stage yet.

"Another reason why the place is so busy. Meela puts on quite a show," Tennille grins.

Amari takes his attention to the stage and gets comfortable. A large, good-looking brother wearing a tuxedo steps on stage, holding out his hand. A smaller, dainty hand uses its fingers to walk along his palm before grasping it, and out comes Jamila. She looks gorgeous, sexy, alluring, captivating—she's all of that and then some. She looks exactly like Josephine, too. The hair, or wig, is in an Eton crop style.

"That's her signature hairdo," Tennille whispers.

She has on a banana skirt and glittery pasties covering her nipples.

Her breasts look delectable...and her thighs...and her stomach. Shit, her whole body.

Amari tells himself not to drool but damned if his mouth is listening. Jamila opens her mouth and sings the first few notes of "J'ai Deux Amours," and Amari is instantly transported to 1920's Paris. Jamila looks out to the audience and finds him instantly. She licks her lips and winks at him. She returns her attention to the gentleman on stage as they dance together as he joins in to sing the man's part. He might as well be on mute because all Amari can hear is Jamila's siren song.

When the performance ends, Amari is on his feet cheering loudly with the rest of the crowd. Tennille looks at him with a knowing smile.

"Shut up," he teases.

The other ladies take to the stage one after another but none of them can hold a candle to Jamila. Amari can hear Jamila's sweet voice throughout the entire night. He was a fool to think that he could come here, see that striking enchantress, then simply go home. Jamila is a dream he doesn't want to wake up from. While he doesn't want to get played again, for her, he finds himself willing to take the risk.

A couple of hours pass and the cabaret for the most part has cleared out. Amari carefully suggests that he and Tennille wait for Jamila to congratulate her. Racking his brain trying to think of an excuse to see her again, Amari figures asking her to coffee seems too simple now. Hell, he overheard one guy talking about how she turned him down when he offered to take her to Cabo. She would laugh in his face for a coffee invitation.

Jamila walks out in a pair of tight dark blue

jeans, a turquoise button-down blouse, and a pair of black leather ankle boots with a matching jacket. When she sees Tennille and Amari she waves gently, a smirk slightly spreading across her face. As soon as Amari waves back he steps forward to approach her when someone quickly beats him to it.

"Hi, Jamila."

"Hi, Frank. Did you enjoy the show?"

"You know I always enjoy seeing you. You always light up the stage."

Amari's about two seconds from interrupting this dude's weak ass game. Jamila is clearly just humoring ole boy.

"Well, thank you. I'm glad to hear it."

"Listen, I know you have a boyfriend…"

Boyfriend? Tennille never mentioned a boyfriend, but of course, she has one. A woman like her couldn't possibly be single.

"Frank, you are married, and didn't your wife just have a baby?"

"Yes, but we could be discreet."

Is this motherfucker serious? He has a wife and a baby at home and he's trying to make Jamila his side chick? Nope, that's it.

Amari approaches them. He gives Jamila a warm smile, and Frank a grimace.

"Is everything okay?" Amari asks Jamila.

"We're fine," Frank responds.

"I didn't ask you, nigga."

Amari steps up to Frank who seems to get the picture that Amari's not fucking around and backs away but doesn't leave.

Jamila loops her arm through Amari's and places her hand on his shoulder. She definitely knows the power she wields because Amari immediately calms down.

"I'm sorry, Frank. I can't. Cheating is a no-go for me." Jamila gives him a weak smile.

There's something about Jamila's tone that makes Amari pause. Has she been cheated on? And if so, what was the stupid bastard thinking?

Frank kisses Jamila's hand and takes his leave. Amari gives him a look of warning, and he takes it, leaving even quicker.

"Look at you being all chivalrous," Jamila teases.

"I know you could handle yourself, but I am a protective man. It's just in my nature."

"I appreciate it."

"I suddenly feel silly that I didn't get you any flowers."

"It's okay. Thank you for coming. And I'm sorry

about being at your house a couple of months ago. I don't think I ever apologized for that."

"You're welcome. And no worries about the whole house misunderstanding."

"Thank you so much."

While Tennille chats with Daisy and Cleo, Amari and Jamila stand in awkward silence, stealing glances at one another.

"Ahem," Amari clears his throat, getting himself ready to say something.

"Meela! You were so good up there!" Tennille hugs her.

Really?

It feels like every time Amari is ready to make a move, he's interrupted. Is no one going to let him talk to the woman?

"Thank you, T."

"T, could you give us a minute?" Amari interrupts, if he was going to get any time with her, he'd have to create his own.

"Okay, Uncle Pooh," Tennille mocks. "Take all the time you need. I need another beverage anyway."

Amari lets out a nervous chuckle. "Sorry about her," he says.

"It's fine," Jamila giggles.

"Um, look, I don't want to come off like that guy

Frank. You know, with you having a boyfriend and everything."

"I don't have a boyfriend. I just didn't correct Frank because I wanted him to back off."

"Oh, okay. Well in that case would you like to—"

A slender Afro-Latina woman with golden skin, curly light brown hair, and matching freckles approaches them. "Hey, sorry to interrupt but Meela I have bad news."

Are you fucking kidding me?

"Your landlord found out?" Jamila says, her tone sounding defeated.

"Yeah, he did. He said if you're going to stay then you need to be added to the lease and pay rent. I'm so sorry, babe."

"It's okay, Char. I'll figure something out."

"I'll be on the lookout for anyone looking for a roommate," Char says.

"Thanks. I appreciate it."

She walks away and it's just Amari and Jamila again. She lets out a mournful sigh. Amari hates seeing her look so defeated.

"How much is rent at your friend's place?" Amari asks.

"Way out of my price range. She has three roommates whom all pay an equal share, and it would still cut way into my budget."

Amari watches as the tears form in her eyes. It's hard seeing her so depressed after she was just mesmerizing everyone not two hours ago. Amari doesn't know what to say. Offering his place seems like a logical choice but they still don't know each other well enough for him to do that.

"There's not anyone else here that will let you stay with them?" he asks.

"All of the girls have roommate situations just like Char. Hell, some of them have four or five roommates. I don't want to impose, and they won't have room for me. I mean, there's Cleo but she's a single mom with three kids, and Ms. Liz takes care of her ailing grandmother. Staying with them would be an even bigger imposition. I'm either going to have to live in my car or move back home."

Tennille rejoins them. "Whoa, why do you both look like somebody died?"

"I may have to go back to Nebraska."

"Why?"

"I can't afford to stay here without help and Char can't let me stay with her anymore."

"You can stay with me, Mom, and Grams."

T, you're a genius! Dear lord let her say yes.

"When I suggested that you said your mom would be in my business," Jamila argues.

"And she will, but what choice do you have?"

Amari looks at Jamila as if he's trying to play it cool but he's bursting to beg her to take T up on her offer.

Jamila shrugs her shoulders. "You're right. Let me go get my stuff from Char's and I'll meet you at your grandma's in an hour."

"Great."

Amari and Tennille walk Jamila to her car just in case Frank's lurking somewhere outside.

"Thanks again, T." Jamila hugs her.

"No problem. I'll text you the address."

"Sounds good. I'll see you in a bit, and it was nice seeing you again, Amari."

"You, too."

Jamila waves at them and drives away.

"That was promising," Tennille says.

"What?"

"The little looks you two just gave each other."

"Whatever."

"Uncle Pooh, I need a favor."

"What's up?"

"I need you to help me convince Grandma to let Jamila move in before she gets to the house."

"What!"

"It's not like I had time to tell Grandma. You were standing right there when I suggested it to Jamila."

"Yeah, but according to Jamila you suggested it before. I assumed you spoke to Mom and Ken already, and what am I talking about? Of course, you didn't. What the hell is with you volunteering other folks' homes?"

"Please, help me."

"Ugh! Damnit, T."

"C'mon, you're a mature adult. Grandma will be more likely to say yes if you back me up."

"Fine, but only because Jamila needs help."

"And because you like her."

"Don't push it."

5

AMARI

Thankfully, Amari and Tennille beat Jamila to the house. Amari called his Mom and told her he needed to run something by her when he drops off Tennille. Though Miss Vonetta is a very kind and understanding woman, she's not a fan of having news dropped on her last minute. So, if he wants to win her over, Amari has to be measured in how he approaches this.

He enters the house and is immediately greeted by warmth and the smell of cinnamon. It's been chilly lately and whenever the weather cools down, Vonetta turns up the heater and makes a batch of her famous snickerdoodles. Kenya is upstairs asleep since her shift at LAX starts early in the morning. Vonetta sits on the couch rewatching *Attack on the*

Pentagon for the millionth time. She has a thing for action movies.

"Hey, you two. How was karaoke?"

"They didn't have karaoke this time, but we still had fun. Jamila gave an amazing performance, Grandma. She did a homage to Josephine Baker."

"I'm sorry I missed that. Did she wear a banana skirt and everything?"

"Yep, even wore her hair like her."

"That sounds like a good time. Ya'll hungry?" Vonetta asks as she heads to the kitchen.

"Yes, ma'am," Amari and Tennille both reply.

Tennille nudges Amari with her elbow and he frowns at her. She gestures for him to say something to Vonetta.

He mouths, "Not yet."

"Then when? Do it now. Meela will be here any minute," Tennille whispers.

"What y'all whispering about?" Vonetta asks carrying a plate full of food for each of them.

"Huh?" They both say looking guilty as sin.

"What's going on?"

"You see momma..." Amari starts. "Um. You know how you raised us to always look out for others?"

"Yes," Vonetta answers looking confused.

"Well, what had happened... You know, Jamila?" Tennille says.

"Yes, we were just talking about her a second ago."

"Yeah, well um. Her ex-boyfriend cheated on her and kicked her out of the apartment they shared."

"Oh my, that's a shame. Ya'll come on. Sit down and eat."

Amari and Tennille take a seat. Tennille's phone buzzes and Amari sees a text from Jamila.

On my way. Thanks again, T!

Shit! They have got to get this out in the open. No more pussyfooting.

"Momma, Jamila needs a place to stay, and in an effort to help a friend, your overzealous grand-daughter..."

"Tennille Heather Ann Sanders, did you tell that child she could stay here?"

"Kind of. Grandma, please! Jamila's a nice person and she needs help. She'll pay rent and she'll make herself useful around the house. Please. We have plenty of room—"

"*We* do not have anything. I have plenty of room. This is my house, young lady. You'd be smart to remember that."

"Yes, ma'am."

Vonetta lets out a sigh. "Look, I'll think about it. Ask her if she can come by next week. I'd like to actually speak with her before I agree to anything."

Just then the doorbell rings.

"Who the hell could be coming by at this of time night?" Vonetta gets up to answer the door.

"No, Momma. Let me get it." Amari gets up and opens the door.

Jamila offers him a bright, spellbinding grin. "Hello again, Amari."

"Hi, Jamila." Amari smiles back temporarily forgetting his mom and Tennille's presence.

"Pooh Bear, who's at the door?" Vonetta asks.

Amari turns to his mother opening the door wider. Jamila takes it as her cue to come in.

"Hello, Mrs. Hawkins." Jamila offers Vonetta a warm hug. "I can't thank you enough for letting me stay here. It's so kind of you. I thought I was going to have to go back to Nebraska."

Vonetta looks at Tennille like she's going to choke her. Amari steps in.

"Jamila, Tennille was just telling my mother how you would be happy to pay rent and assist around the house."

"Oh, of course! I don't have a lot of money to offer but I can pay you five hundred dollars a month for a room, and I can cook or clean. Whichever you prefer, ma'am," Jamila says.

Jamila's voice sounds jittery. Clearly, his mother's reaction to her popping over unannounced isn't lost on her. Amari already knows his mother's answer, and it won't be good news for Jamila. Feeling sorry for her dilemma, Amari reaches over and takes Jamila's hand giving her a sympathetic squeeze. Jamila looks up at him and smiles sweetly, obviously appreciating the gesture. They're soon transported back into the little bubble they briefly inhabited when he opened the door. Amari rubs his thumb over the top of Jamila's hand as she gazes at him.

"She can stay," Vonetta announces.

"She can?" Amari asks, desperately trying to not sound too excited.

"Of course. I'm not about to force this poor child to pack up and go back home," Vonetta replies.

"Oh my God! Thank you so much." Jamila hugs Vonetta again.

"You're welcome, sugar."

"Thank you, Grandma." Tennille smiles.

"You be quiet. You're still on my shit list."

Tennille looks down, avoiding eye contact.

"Pooh Bear, go help Jamila get her stuff out the

car and show her to Iman's old room." Vonetta orders.

"Yes, Momma."

Jamila opens the door to the back seat of her car. "I don't know how much help I need. I only have a couple of bags."

"You take one and I'll take the other," Amari replies.

When they go back into the house Amari sees Vonetta giving Tennille a lecture in the backyard. Being who she is, she took it outside so she could raise her voice without waking Kenya. Amari looks behind him and sees Jamila staring at the scene wide-eyed.

"Just keep walking and don't look," Amari advises.

"I feel bad like I got Tennille in trouble."

"You didn't. Tennille got Tennille in trouble."

Amari opens the door to what used to be his eldest sister's room. Vonetta keeps it looking nice in case Iman, Zuri, and their families visit.

"This is nice. I'm guessing Iman is another sister."

"Yes, ma'am. T didn't mention her?"

"No, she mainly talked about her mom and your mom. Every now and then she'd bring you up, but it was only in passing."

"What did she say about me?"

"Not much. Just that the two of you hung out a lot but that the cabaret really wasn't your scene."

"Oh, so she just threw my Black ass completely under the bus."

"Yes, sir, she did," and they share a laugh.

"Well as you may have noticed tonight, the cabaret is most definitely my scene."

"Is that so?"

"That is so."

Jamila bites her bottom lip. She clears her throat and starts to unpack. "So, Kenya, Iman, and you."

"And Zuri."

"Another sibling?"

"Another sister."

"Three sisters and you're the only boy."

"Yep, and the youngest."

"They must have spoiled you."

"Yes and no. They spoiled me but also terrorized me."

Jamila giggles.

Amari continues. "It's all good though. I love my sisters."

"And look at it this way, between your sisters,

your mom, Tennille, and Ms. Yolanda, you're surrounded by so many incredible women."

"Yes, I am," Amari smirks. "And the list seems to be growing."

He grins at Jamila who now looks flushed.

"I'm going to let you go ahead and get settled. I'll be seeing you, Jamila."

"Meela. All my friends call me Meela."

Amari nods. "Mine call me Mar."

"Goodnight, Mar."

"Goodnight, Meela."

6

JAMILA

It's been a month since Jamila has been staying with the Hawkins and it's been a hoot. She and Vonetta cook together and sing gospel much to the annoyance and amusement of Kenya and Tennille. And Kenya has been nothing less than the biggest sweetheart. Yes, she's a bit nosy but it's not from being overbearing—unlike how she is with Tennille—it's mainly from boredom. All Kenya really does is work and come home. Jamila promised to take her to the cabaret when they both have a day off so she can meet the other girls. And Mar...his fine ass has been by the house almost every day since she moved in. He's even helped out in the kitchen a few times.

While she hasn't had a lot of time alone with

him, all that changed last Sunday. Vonetta was at church, Kenya was at work, and Tennille stayed over at a friend's house, so Jamila slept in after working until midnight the night before. She got up and went straight to the bathroom to get ready for the day. She tried not to take too long, but after having to take showers at Char's place that varied from lukewarm to downright freezing, Jamila was happy to finally take a long, hot shower. She got out about twenty minutes later and heard the front door open. Thinking it was one of the ladies, she made her way back to her room to moisturize. That's when she heard his voice.

"Anybody home?"

"I'm up here, Mar," she called out.

She heard him make his way upstairs and before she knew it, the door was opening with his large frame in the doorway. The only thing covered on Jamila was her hair, wrapped in a towel.

"Hi Mar," she'd squeaked.

Amari's eyes were the size of saucers. "I'm so sorry, Mm—Mm—Meela."

Amari turned, and in his flustered state, he smacked himself in the face with the door as he tried to exit and close it at the same time.

"Ow! Fuck," he'd screamed.

Clearly embarrassed, he ambled away still trying to find his balance.

Jamila quickly threw on a fitted t-shirt and boy shorts to see if Amari was okay. She found him seated in the hallway, leaning against the wall, holding his nose.

"Mar, are you okay?"

"Uh, not really."

"Oh, let me get you a towel."

Jamila rushed to the bathroom and grabbed a towel, moistening it with cold water. She lowered his hand and placed the towel under his nose.

"I'm sorry, Mar."

"Why are you apologizing? I'm the one who walked in on you."

"Yeah, but I didn't tell you I was naked."

"Why were you naked?"

"I had just gotten out the shower."

"Oh." He flipped the towel over before placing it back under his nose. "I thought Ken, T, or momma would be home by now."

"Ken is working overtime, your mom volunteered to help with the church bake sale after today's service, and Tennille's at a friend's place."

"So, it's just you and me?" he asked.

"Yep. Just the two of us," she smiled.

"That was never my favorite Bill Withers song," Amari joked.

Jamila giggled.

"Sorry, that was a bad joke. Just trying to alleviate my embarrassment." He looked down.

Jamila took his chin and raised his head so they were eye-to-eye.

"You have nothing to be embarrassed by. And my favorite song of his is 'Lovely Day.'"

"Mine's 'Ain't No Sunshine.'" Amari smiled.

"That's a good one."

Amari chuckled and then cleared his throat. "You don't seem embarrassed at all."

"Should I be?" Jamila sat next to him.

"I mean, some people might get embarrassed if someone they barely knew saw them naked."

"Some people don't look as good naked as I do," she retorted. "Wouldn't you agree?"

"Umm," he blushed.

"What? You got a good enough look," she teased.

"Can we change the subject?"

"Fine, but I will say this. I showed you mine so one of these days, you'll have to show me yours. It's only fair."

"I'll think about it."

"You do that."

They'd spent the remainder of the day watching movies, talking, and joking around. Amari ordered some Chinese for when the family got home, and thankfully his nose felt better after he put some ice on it. Kenya came home first followed by Tennille. When Vonetta came home and saw Amari's face, he explained what happened and she examined him to make sure his nose wasn't broken. That's how Jamila found out she was a retired nurse. When it was clear Amari would be okay, he and Jamila told everyone the whole story and his family proceeded to laugh at him. He had a good laugh about it, too.

They had a nice dinner. Being around the Hawkins family felt right. Especially spending time with Amari. Being around him was...

"Jamila Washington."

The casting assistant calls her name and Jamila is awakened from her daydream. She shouldn't have been thinking about Amari anyway. She's not quite three months out of her relationship with Barry. Besides, she's supposed to be focusing on her audition.

"I'm here," Jamila responds.

"Come with me."

Jamila gets up and follows the young woman who can't be more than thirty but looks like she's still in high school. She has mousy brown hair and freckles. She's dressed in jeans and a striped button-down shirt.

"I'm Amanda, the casting associate. You'll be reading for the part of Aurora in front of the director, the casting director—my boss—and the producer. I'll be the person reading Helene's part. Got it?"

"Got it."

"Great. Just go in and break a leg."

"Thanks."

The audition room looks like any other audition room she's been in over the past three years. A plain, nondescript room with white walls and a long table with the creative team behind it. Jamila's an anomaly in this industry. She'd quickly signed with an agent after she moved and has received fairly steady work ever since. Even when work is slow, she has residual checks to help her get by. That's pretty unheard of for a newcomer. Especially a Black woman.

"Hello," Jamila greets them.

"Please start when you're ready," the director says.

While Amanda never specified who was who, after being in L.A. for all this time, it isn't hard for Jamila to suss out who's a director, writer, or producer.

"Helene, what are you doing out here?"

"Just thinking," Amanda says with zero emotion.

That's always been something that annoyed Jamila. Would it kill the creative team to bring in an actor for auditions? She always feels like she's talking to a robot.

"Thinking about what?" Jamila centers in on Amanda.

"Mom and Dad."

"They would be so proud of you." Jamila smiles.

"You think?"

"Of course. You were their wunderkind." Jamila lets out a humorless chuckle.

"Not this again."

"Not what?"

"This weird obsession you have that mom and dad didn't love you. It's getting old, Aurora."

"That's easy for you to say. You were their white birth child, not the Black kid they adopted to convince themselves they were *good* white people."

"Thank you," the director says.

"Thank you," Jamila replies warmly.

Hours later she's at home sitting on her bed going over a script for a commercial she shoots in a couple of days. There is a knock on the door.

"Come in."

Amari enters with his eyes covered.

"Very funny, Mr. Hawkins."

He uncovers his eyes and laughs. "How did your audition go?"

"I think it went well."

"Cool. Are you busy right now?"

"Just going over lines."

"You want some help?"

"Sure." Jamila pats the spot next to her on the bed.

He takes a seat and skims the script. "Who am I playing?"

"It clearly says 'husband' and 'wife', Mar." Jamila playfully rolls her eyes.

"What? You might want to do one of those Meisner exercises where we switch roles or something."

"I don't think that's part of the Meisner technique."

"You should come up with something like that. You can call it the Washington technique."

Jamila laughs. "Everybody will think it's Denzel's."

"Or Kerry's," Amari jokes.

"Shut up," Jamila giggles. "You going to help me or what?"

"Okay. No more jokes."

Jamila reads the first line, "Hey, you."

"Hey," Amari replies sounding almost as robotic as Amanda did.

"Mar, I'm your wife. Sound like you're happy to see me."

"Yes, Ms. Duvernay."

"First off, I would be Ms. Prince-Bythewood or Ms. Lemmons. Thank you very much. And second, we're starting from the top."

Amari lets out a chuckle that makes Jamila's pussy tingle.

"Hey, you." Jamila looks at Amari.

He looks up at her like she's a prize. "Hey."

"You look hungry."

"I'm starving."

"I got something for you to eat."

Jamila notices that Amari's face is closer to hers than it was a second ago.

"Good. I can't wait."

They're so close that if Jamila moved an inch forward, their lips would meet.

What the fuck am I doing? His mom is letting me stay here, so in return, I make out with her son? Get it together, Meela.

Jamila backs away. "Um…then it says that I pull the fast-food bag from behind my back." Jamila reads the stage direction.

"Oh, right." Amari laughs nervously before finding his bearings. "Wait. This is a fast-food commercial?"

"Yeah. It's for that burger joint, Bear Burgers. You know 'for when you're hungry as a bear.'"

"I have never eaten there."

"Why?"

"On pure principle. The concept is just ignorant. A bear as a mascot for a burger joint? And what the hell is up with the suggestive dialogue?"

"I don't know. Sex sells."

"Burgers?"

"Apparently. C'mon, didn't this make you want to eat a burger?" Jamila smiles.

"No, Meela. Not a burger," Amari replies with that unfairly sexy, husky ass voice.

It's her fault. Meela flirted with him after the naked incident and invited him into her room to go over lines that are entirely too arousing for a burger commercial, but it ends now. She and Amari are friends and nothing more.

The doorbell rings.

"That's probably Mrs. Gordon's granddaughter," Jamila remarks.

"What do you think she's going to ask to borrow now?"

"Who knows? Yesterday it was ketchup. C'mon, who the fuck borrows ketchup from their neighbor?"

Mrs. Gordon is still determined to get her granddaughter, Shannon, hooked up with Amari. Nosy as she is, she noticed Jamila had moved in, so in an effort to find out more about Vonetta's new house guest, she's been sending Shannon next door to "borrow" things from the Hawkins' house. Jamila finds the whole thing funny. She and Amari have made a game of guessing what she'll ask for each time she comes by.

"I think it will be flour," Amari guesses.

"I'm going to go with mayonnaise. I think they're going to keep going with the condiment theme."

"Ah! Wise choice. Let's go find out."

The two of them arrive downstairs just as Vonetta opens the door. This time it's Shannon and Mrs. Gordon.

"Hey, Bertha. How are you and Shannon doing?"

"We're fine. Shannon dear, isn't there something you wanted to ask Amari?"

"Not really, Grandma."

Jamila feels so sorry for Shannon. It's obvious Mrs. Gordon is trying to pawn the poor girl off on some unsuspecting man. Unfortunately for Shannon, while she is pretty, she's also as dull as a box of rocks. A few days ago, Jamila got dragged into a conversation with her and all she yammered about was Atlanta and how much she misses it. This girl clearly doesn't want to be here and is only humoring her grandmother. Someone needs to remind her she's a grown-ass woman and can hop on a plane and go back home anytime she wants.

"C'mon now, dear," Mrs. Gordon insists.

"Amari, would you like to escort me to the church function next weekend?" Shannon mumbles while looking at her feet.

"Uh, um...I'm sorry, what?" Amari stammers.

"Okay so not flour or mayonnaise," Jamila mumbles.

"Oh, Shannon, honey. That's not going to be possible. You see Amari and Jamila are dating," Vonetta replies.

"Oh. When did this happen?" Mrs. Gordon asks.

Yeah, I would love to know that too.

"It's been going on for a while, but they finally made it official two weeks ago. Amari got to know Jamila through Tennille, and with her staying here, things just blossomed. Isn't that right, kids?" Vonetta smiles.

"Yes," Amari replies without hesitation.

Jamila nods. "Like a rose."

"That would explain why you've been coming over here so much," Mrs. Gordon says to Amari.

"I wouldn't say I've been over here that much," Amari argues.

"Yeah, you have," Kenya retorts. "And we all know it's been to see your woman."

Jamila tries not to laugh while Amari stares daggers at Kenya. Of course, she would use her mom's lie to poke fun at him.

"Well, I have prayed on it, and I know that Amari and my Shannon are meant to be."

God must have her listed as "never answer" 'cause there's no way that's happening.

"If things don't work out between you and Jamila —and I suspect they won't—then you will let me know?"

Is this lady serious? She's trying to jack my fake boyfriend right in front of me.

Jamila wraps her arm around Amari's midsection and squeezes. He pulls her in closer.

"I don't think that's going to be happening anytime soon, Mrs. Gordon, but if Mar's single friends are interested, we'll get back to you." Jamila gives her best fake smile, and Amari chuckles.

Mrs. Gordon shoots Jamila a vicious glare. "Come along, Shannon."

As soon as Mrs. Gordon and Shannon are out of earshot, Amari whips around to his mother.

"Momma, what was that?" Amari asks.

"That, my boy, was me saving your ass."

"I could have handled that."

"Really, Mr. Uh Um..." Kenya laughs.

"Shut up, Ken."

"I may have saved you today, but you two are going to have to play up this new relationship."

"Why? She now thinks we're together. That's not enough?" Jamila asks.

"Not hardly. Bertha is nosier than a motherfucker," Vonetta says.

"Sure is," Kenya agrees. "Her late husband was a detective, and she took that shit way too seriously. Has been in everyone's business for years."

"So, what does that mean?" Jamila asks.

"You two better start acting booed up," Kenya says as she heads to the kitchen.

Jamila looks at Amari. He shrugs and gives a sweet smile.

So much for friends and nothing more.

7

AMARI

mari stands in the conference room at Echo's and watches LaWanda King shake hands with the CEO, Martin Campbell. Amari did it! Adrenaline courses through his body and he's tempted to hop in his car, drive up to the mountains, and wrestle a bear. At this moment, Amari feels like he can do anything. He secured the rights to LaWanda's novel, making this another huge win for Echo, and he can't wait to celebrate. Martin heads toward the door after saying his goodbyes to LaWanda and the rest of the team. He then stops in front of Amari.

"Great work, Amari," Martin says, gripping Amari's hand firmly.

"Thank you, Martin."

"Let's meet next week to discuss adding 'senior' to your title."

"Are we discussing this hypothetically? Or is this a done deal?"

"This is more than a done deal, Hawkins. You have just secured us what will no doubt be our highest-rated original program to date. We'll make a formal announcement, but I want to make sure that you and I meet alone beforehand."

"Sounds great! Thank you." Martin pats Amari on his shoulder before heading out the door.

Amari grins so hard his face hurts. He punches the air.

That's what I'm talking about!

"What are you so happy about?" LaWanda teases as she approaches him.

"Ms. King, you have just given me the keys to the kingdom."

"Happy to do it. I can't tell you how pleased I am to be working with Echo. I don't even want to tell you about some of the nonsense and lowballing the other streaming services put me through."

"I can only imagine. Probably treated you like you just fell off the turnip truck instead of a multi-award-winning author."

"Chile, you have no idea. One of those folks

suggested making the main character white," LaWanda turned her nose up. It wasn't hard to see how insulting that suggestion was.

"They wanted to cast a white woman in a movie about a young woman's journey of finding herself in 1970's Detroit? In a neighborhood called Little Africa?"

"Yes."

"Jesus Christ."

"Even he could not have helped them." They share a laugh.

"Now that it's official, I want you to come to a gathering I'm having to celebrate our partnership," LaWanda says.

"You knew you were going to go with Echo from jump, didn't you?"

"I will neither confirm nor deny."

"Uh huh. Had to make sure you collected that bag, huh?"

"No comment," LaWanda smiles. "You should come. Lots of literary folks will be in attendance along with quite a few actors and other artists I'm also friends with."

"May I bring someone?"

"Of course."

As much as Amari believes Tennille would

benefit from going to the party given her major, he knows exactly who he's going to take.

It's Friday night, and Amari's chilling in a recliner, sipping a beer at Keith's house while they watch the Rams play.

"I'm still tripping over your mom lying to that woman and her poor granddaughter."

"Do not feel sorry for them. Mrs. Gordon just kept pushing Shannon to interact with me even though it was obvious––very quickly––that neither of us was interested."

"Why did she keep going if there was no spark between y'all?"

"Because Mrs. Gordon is stubborn as hell. She thinks God wants me and Shannon together."

"Oh, okay. So, she crazy."

"She's just old school."

"Is Layla still calling you?"

"Yessir! And I'm still avoiding her."

"Shit, Mar. You swimming in women, my nigga." Keith chuckles. "You got the neighbor chick, your ex, and a fake girlfriend. And you wanted to be alone."

"Yep. Might as well be talking to a brick wall... but if I'm being real, only one of them actually has my interest."

"I'm guessing it's a certain new roommate at Ms. Vonetta's crib."

"That is correct."

"You done already seen her naked. Go ahead and make that move, my boy."

"Who has Mar seen naked?" Erika asks entering the man cave.

"I accidentally saw Jamila naked a while back. It's no big deal."

Erica raised her eyebrows, humorously looking at Amari. "I'd say it is. How did that happen?"

"I came by the house, and it looked empty, so I asked if anyone was home and she said she was. I went upstairs and her door was ajar, I thought it was cool to open it, so I did, and that's when I saw her."

"You owe her an apology." Erika playfully pops Amari upside the head.

"Watch it. I did apologize and, honestly, she wasn't mad or embarrassed. As a matter of fact, she said I owed her a peek of my goods."

"Maybe you'll get a chance to give her one when you take her to LaWanda's party," Keith says.

"I don't know, man."

"Why? I thought you were feeling her?"

"I am, but I don't want her to think I'm using my

title to get her into bed. She's an actress, and I don't want to seem like I'm doing some predatory shit."

"I feel you. That makes sense."

"I'm taking her so she can meet some folks and do some networking. I don't want her to think she owes me anything. So, for now, we're just friends."

"Unless you're around Mrs. Gordon."

"Hell, even then, all we ever do is hold hands and give each other pecks. Mrs. Gordon's in her seventies. It's not like we're trying to give her a show."

"I think you're right to be careful, Amari. But just remember this, no woman is okay with showing off her goods and asking to see yours if she's not feeling you. You might want to go ahead and make that move."

She gives Keith a kiss and heads toward the door. "I'm going to the store. Ya'll want anything?"

"I'm good," Amari replies.

"Bring me back a pint of Ben and Jerry's, baby."

"Okay. I'll be back. Love you." Erica blows Keith a kiss.

"Love you more." He winks at her, and Erika leaves the room, closing the door tight behind her.

Amari sees how much his best friend loves his wife and can't help but feel a little jealous. He's definitely happy for Keith, but since he's met Jamila, he's realized how much he's been missing by avoiding relationships. Joking around with her has been great, and he hasn't stopped thinking about how they almost kissed when he helped her with her lines. Things with Layla were fun and easy at first, too. And Jamila just left a fucked-up situation with her ex.

No matter how he feels about Amari, he can't lose sight of the fact that they both aren't ready for anything more. Their fake boyfriend and girlfriend act is strictly that, an act. It won't ever go past that. It can't.

8

JAMILA

Jamila tries to sit still while Charmaine does her makeup, but she's so excited and nervous that her knees keep shaking.

"Girl, if you don't stop, I'ma end up poking you in the eye with this pencil," Charmaine complains.

"Sorry, Char, but I still can't believe Mar invited me to a party at LaWanda King's house. I read *Just an Ordinary Girl* three times. I would kill to even have a small part in the adaptation."

"Sweetie, it's going to be on Echo. Just ask Amari to hook you up."

"I can't do that."

"Why not?" Cleo asks as she plugs in a thermal

stove for the flat iron. "I mean, what are fake boyfriends for?"

"They're not for being taken advantage of, I know that much. Mar is a great guy, and he's a good friend. I don't want him to think I'm only cool with him for my career."

"Meela, please. You are more than cool with him," Cleo says.

"What's that supposed to mean?"

"You wanna fuck that man so bad, it's crazy," Char says.

"What? No, I don't!" Jamila says not sounding remotely convincing.

"Baby, you're a better actress than that. Try delivering that line again." Cleo laughs.

"Fuck you," Jamila joins in, cackling.

"For real though, Meela, it's obvious you're feeling Mar, and Daisy told me how he was looking at you when he came to the Kitten Heel. You should go for it."

"I just got out of a relationship."

"Ugh! Barry was a lack of good judgment, not a boyfriend. Besides, you and Amari don't have to date. You can just fuck. A lot," Char asserts.

She puts the finishing touches on Jamila's makeup while Cleo does her hair.

"He is fine," Cleo agrees.

"As hell," Char adds.

There's a knock on the door.

"Come in," they say in unison.

Amari struts in wearing a sharp red wine suit paired with a black collared, button-down shirt. His hair is freshly cut with a low fade connected to his low-trimmed beard. His strong body fills out the suit *very* well. All three ladies look at him with their mouths agape.

"Y'all okay?" he smiles.

"Meela, if you don't fuck him, I will. To hell with a girl code," Char mumbles.

Even though she knew Char was joking, Jamila felt the urge to smack the taste out of Char's overly perfect mouth. Char gives her a look that says, *try it.*

Jamila turns back to address Amari. "We're fine."

"And so are you." Cleo winks at him.

Amari grins and looks down in embarrassment. "Thank you, Cleo." Though he's talking to Cleo, all his attention is on Jamila, flashing her a warm smile. "Just wanted to see if you're almost ready. The car will be here soon."

"You're not driving? If you don't want to I can," Jamila says.

"No need. LaWanda's husband is sending cars for all of the guests."

LaWanda King's husband, Christian, is a millionaire who works in finance and has supported her for years until her writing career popped off. He's her biggest fan. Jamila has always admired their relationship. That man is the antithesis of Barry. Amari shares a lot of Christian's qualities, which means he is destined to make an amazing husband.

What the hell am I thinking?

She's just told the girls doing anything romantic with Amari is out of the question. But is it really?

"I'll be down in a sec. I just need to get dressed." Jamila smiles.

"Okay. See you in a bit," Amari says winking back.

After Char finishes with Jamila's hair and makeup, she takes off her robe and puts on the strapless dress she splurged on when she went shopping with Kenya and Tennille. Tennille picked the dress. First off, it was too expensive and maybe too revealing but of course, they outvoted her. It is a gorgeous dress. It's a black figure-hugging maxi dress with holes cut out down the front. With the makeup, hair, and dress, Jamila looks like a sexy vixen.

Jamila makes her way downstairs with Char and Cleo behind her. Amari is chatting with Vonetta when she smiles at Jamila who is behind him. Amari turns around and his eyes travel up her body, and when he lands on her face, she takes a deep breath. He looks at her and shakes his head. He might as well have stripped her down right there because that look could only mean one thing, he wants to devour her. This man is going to be her undoing.

When they arrive at the party, it's nothing less than glamour. There's a red carpet, lights, and flashing cameras everywhere. A few folks come out of cars in front of them, walking the carpet to have their picture taken beside a large beautiful rose bush serving as the background. When it's Jamila and Amari's turn, the photographer grins at them. The photographer is a pretty, petite Black woman with locs styled in a top bun wearing a gorgeous champagne-colored V-neck dress.

"You two are the flyest looking couple so far. Don't tell Christian and LaWanda I said that," she winks.

Jamila and Amari laugh, and neither bothers to correct her. Amari wraps his arm around Jamila's waist and pulls her to him. The camera flashes and the photographer shows them the pics. If anyone who didn't know them saw these, they would think she and Amari were relationship goals.

"Let's do some more. I want to get a few with the two of you looking at each other," the photographer requests.

Jamila looks into Amari's eyes, feeling what little resolve she has left melting.

God, he has such beautiful, soulful, kind eyes. I could tell this man anything and he wouldn't hurt me. Why am I fighting my attraction to him?

Jamila wishes she could read Amari's mind because the way he's looking at her tells her he may be thinking the same thing.

"Hey, fly couple!" The photographer laughs. Jamila and Amari look over at her. "Other people want to get their pics taken, too."

She nods toward a line that has formed behind them.

"Sorry." Amari blushes as the folks behind them grin in amusement.

He offers Jamila his arm. She takes it, and they enter the party.

"Thank you again for inviting me, Mar."

"My pleasure. Auditions are important but so is networking."

"I know. I never get to chat with industry folks that aren't starving artists like me."

Amari smiles. "I'm glad I could help."

The DJ posted up near the bar plays "Sweet Lady" by Tyrese.

"Do you want to dance?" Jamila asks.

"Let's do it," Amari answers.

They take to the dance floor and hold each other close.

"Amari?"

"Yes."

"Why didn't we correct the photographer?"

"I don't know. I guess it didn't seem important."

"Are you sure that's the only reason?" Jamila whispers.

Amari pulls her closer and gazes at her. His hands squeeze her waist as hers run down his chest. Unsure of what she's doing, Jamila feels the urge to admit that she feels there's something between them, and from her experience, it's not going away. Amari cups her face and lowers his. Their faces are just as close as they were when they ran lines in her bedroom.

"Meela I…"

"Mar!" A woman comes up to them and reaches out to hug Amari.

"Hey, Shai! How are you?"

"I'm great. You'll never guess who I ran into," the lady says enthusiastically. "Layla! She got promoted at the firm. She told me she's been trying to reach out to you, so I gave her your cell number. I hope that was okay."

Jamila looks at Amari and the lustful look he was giving her is long gone. Shai must realize that she's fucked up because she mumbles something about catching up later before making herself scarce.

"Mar..." Jamila begins.

"I'm going to get a drink."

Amari stomps off to the bar while Jamila stands there like Boo Boo the Fool. Nothing like a nice, cold dose of reality to ruin a perfect moment.

Amari is the only person she knows here. Although Jamila recognizes more than a few faces, she decides it would be weird to approach anyone. She makes her way to the backyard where some folks are congregating by the pool.

The home is beautiful. It's a Mediterranean coastal estate that's surprisingly private. No one but the party guests have been milling around. Jamila spots another bar set up by the pool and makes her across the terrace. She wants to give Amari space right now. He's obviously pissed, but the truth is, she's a little pissed, too. Sure, he's upset, but did he have to leave her like that? Jamila doesn't know much about Layla except she's his ex and it ended rather abruptly. Apparently, Amari proposed but the wedding was called off before it could even be planned. Kenya told Jamila that no one knows what prompted the breakup, just that Amari hasn't really been the same since.

Jamila is deep in thought about how she should approach Amari after the awkward interaction with Shai.

He looked like he wanted to be alone but maybe I should check on him.

Right as she's about to head back inside, someone takes a seat at the bar right next to her. Amari can wait. She is here to network, and it would seem rude to just up and leave right as they sat down.

"Are you having a good time?"

When Jamila turns her attention to the person next to her, she nearly falls off her seat. It's LaWanda King.

9
───

AMARI

*A*mari sips his drink, attempting to calm himself before he goes looking for Jamila. He knows he shouldn't have left her the way he did, but he was so pissed. How the fuck do you just give someone's number away without checking with them first? And to their ex-fiancée of all people? Shai is cool people, but she also doesn't have an ounce of common sense.

Honestly, that's not fair. Like most people, she has no clue why he and Layla ended things. Amari has always made it sound like their breakup was mutual and amicable. There is no way Shai could have known how badly Layla fucked up. At the time, Amari was just trying to save face. He didn't want to tell anyone the truth. It was too painful and frankly, embarrassing. Now, he doesn't know what to do. Getting closure would be nice, and now that Layla has his cell number, he may have a chance at getting some. But is it worth reopening an old wound?

The party is packed, and as Amari makes his way through the room, he suddenly hears the sweet voice that hypnotized him only a few months ago.

"Jamila," he breathes.

She's not talking but singing. He makes his way to her, again lured by her siren song. She's captivating the crowd with a stirring, soulful rendition of "Good Morning Heartache" by Billie Holiday. She leans against the piano as a brother grinning at her—a bit too much for Amari's liking—plays. To say she looks sexy would be an understatement. Jamila is provocative without even trying. When they were in the bedroom rehearsing that day, he was going to kiss her, but she pulled back. Thank God things have changed because earlier tonight, she was all in. Why else would she ask him about not correcting the photographer? The real reason he didn't was that it'd felt good having her on his arm and having someone think this bewitchingly gorgeous and witty woman was his.

The crowd erupts in a thunderous applause and Amari joins them, not taking his eyes off Jamila. She catches him staring at her and winks. He winks back and mouths, "You're amazing." She smiles and bites her lip.

"Amari, where have you been hiding her?" LaWanda asks sneaking up behind him.

"Haven't been hiding her anywhere, Ms. King."

"In that case, you absolutely have to bring her to the next gathering. Robert's having a private viewing of the next *Attack on...* movie." LaWanda points to Robert Emerson, Academy Award winner and star of the *Attack on...* series.

Damn. Amari's only ever seen him in passing. Word is he's a major asshole but that hasn't stopped Vonetta from seeing every movie in the franchise. She's going to be so excited when Amari tells her he saw him.

"There will be a private afterparty at The Basement. Everyone will be there."

The Basement is a club co-owned by Robert and model Curtis Brown. It's the spot most of Black Hollywood goes to after a premiere to mingle. It's been the place to be seen after every Image, Soul Train, and BET awards show for years. Amari's definitely taking Jamila, and based on the way things are going, she may end up securing her own invite. She's currently laughing and chatting it up with popular filmmaker Kyle Townsend. Kyle's the homie. Amari discovered him a few years back when he directed an indie film that took Sundance by storm. He then brought that attention to Echo where he directed several episodes of *Sisterhood*, and Amari has dropped his name a few times to direct *Just an Ordinary Girl*. To see Kyle chatting with Jamila makes Amari feel accomplished. This is why he brought her, so others in the industry can see just how special she is. He knew she'd come to the party and work her magic. Hyped by all the excitement, Amari's run-in with Shai is now a distant memory.

"You two make a great couple," LaWanda remarks.

Amari smiles shyly. "We're just friends."

"That may be the case for now but from the way you two were looking at each other and from all the glowing things she's told me about you, it won't be that way for long."

LaWanda walks away to work the room, and Amari turns his attention back to Jamila. She's now chatting with Kyle, actress Tisha Moore, and R&B songstress Chantel Stone. Jamila scans the room until she finds Amari and gestures for him to join them. Amari smiles and heads over, and when he reaches the group, Jamila pulls on his arm.

"We're about to take a picture, Mar. You have to be in it," Jamila smiles.

"Yeah, Mar. Mr. Senior VP!" Tisha chimes in.

"You know we need to work on something else together soon?" Kyle adds.

"I'm working on it, bruh," Amari grins.

Tisha grabs the attention of one of the servers and asks him to take the picture with her phone. They all huddle up and smile for the camera. Amari has his arm draped around Jamila's waist while she leans into him, wrapping her arms around his midsection and resting her head on his chest.

After taking the picture, the two become inseparable. Amari introduces Jamila to countless screenwriters and directors, and by the end of the night, they've danced until their feet hurt.

"Let's go to the garden," Amari suggests, leading Jamila further into the property. From the garden, they can hear the beach, and the ocean is so relaxing as they stand listening to the waves crashing.

"Thank you for bringing me here," Jamila breathes.

She stands in front of his body, leaning into him with her ass brushing against his dick. Amari tries to chill, but the combination of her scent and her closeness is about to do him in.

"You're welcome, Meela."

The cool night air makes Jamila shiver, and she rubs her bare arms.

"Are you cold?"

"A little chilly, but I'll be fine."

"Naw, I got you."

Amari takes off his jacket and drapes it around her. He wraps his arms around her to make sure she's warm. She snuggles up to him as he places a kiss on her head. He's never been happier than in this moment.

Hours later, the car service drops them off at Vonetta's. By that point, they're both starving. Neither of them wants to risk waking anyone up by making something in the kitchen, so they decide to grab a bite elsewhere.

Amari drives, and they talk more during the ride about how much fun they had. Their only complaint being that the food served was good but served in such small portions.

"Let's go to Bear Burger?" Jamila insists.

"What? No. I told you that place is ridiculous."

"Ridiculously good."

"Damn, that was corny."

"Shut up." Jamila playfully hits his shoulder.

"C'mon, please? I booked the commercial, we have to rep the brand."

"Oh, we do, do we?"

"Yes."

"Alright, fine."

They hit up the drive-thru and then go to his house so they won't have to worry about making too much noise.

Taking a seat on the couch, they spread out the food and dig in.

"I swear I thought it would be a dinner party. If I had known it was just appetizers, I would have had us eat dinner beforehand," Amari says, popping a fry into his mouth.

"It's fine. I'm not mad at all," Jamila says, biting her burger.

Amari takes a bite of his burger, and Jamila watches to catch his reaction as he chews it carefully and swallows.

"Alright, it's good," he admits.

"I told you." Jamila laughs.

Jamila takes another bite and lets out a satisfied groan. "Mmm! So good."

She licks some of the special sauce from her lips, and Amari readjusts himself on the couch.

Jamila lets out a long yawn and stretches. "Oh,

sorry. I should head home. I have to get all this makeup off and get into something a little more comfy."

"You should stay here," Amari replies.

Jamila looks surprised by his offer. "I don't want to impose, Mar."

"It's not an imposition. Besides, it's nearly three in the morning. I'm not okay with you taking an Uber this late. I have plenty of room, and I can get you something to wear."

Anxious, Amari scans Jamila's face. If it were up to him, she'd have no choice but to stay.

"Okay fine," Jamila says. "Thanks."

"No problem. Tennille has some hair things she keeps in her room for when she stays over, so you should find a new bonnet and anything else you need in there."

"Great."

Before bed, they clean up. Once they make their way upstairs, Amari rummages through his clothes to find a t-shirt to sleep in. Telling her she can have her pick of any room, she chooses the one next to his, and they bid each other goodnight.

An hour later, Amari lies wide awake in his bed. His mind replays the evening's events and he's filled with a sense of calm. Everything went perfectly despite the earlier hiccup and he did end up having a wonderful time. Having Jamila in his arms while they watched the ocean was both serene and exciting. He wasn't sure about kissing her, no matter how innocent it might have been, but judging by the breath she released, she seemed to enjoy it. He wanted to go further but more guests came out and joined them, not to mention Amari didn't want to overstep any boundaries. Even though they came close to kissing earlier that evening, he still couldn't stop thinking about how she pulled away when they were in her room. She may have had the same reaction if Shai hadn't interrupted them.

A knock on his door gets Amari out of his head.

"Come in, Meela."

She cracks the door open and peeks in. "How did you know it was me?" she teases.

Amari chuckles. "You're the only person here, beautiful."

She looks at him quizzically. They flirted before but he figured complimenting her straight out would give her a better idea of his intentions.

"Thank you, handsome," she smiles.

"What can I do for you?"

"I couldn't sleep, and I was going to ask if I could cuddle up with you."

"Of course. Come here."

Jamila hops into his bed and scoots closer to him.

"Mar?"

"Yeah."

"Before we were interrupted by Shai, were you going to kiss me?"

"I wanted to."

"Oh."

"Is that a bad 'oh' or a good 'oh'?"

"It's a good 'oh.' I actually wanted to kiss you in my room but..."

"But what?"

"I didn't want you to think I was trying to get something from you. Like I was only cool with you so I could get cast in something."

"I would have never thought that, Meela. That's not who you are. You're talented, driven, smart, and charming. Any success you receive will be from your work, not any favors from me or anyone else."

"Thank you. So why haven't you made a move on me?"

"Umm, it's a combination of things. I hold a powerful position and I didn't want you to think I was abusing that power to help you and myself."

"Well as you said, I would never have thought

that because that's not who you are, Amari Hawkins. You're a man of integrity and great character. You're not that guy."

"Thank you."

"You said it was a combination of things, what else is there?"

"Just the bullshit with our exes. You just got out of something, and I'm still dealing with bullshit from my last relationship. I don't want any of our shit to affect anything you and I try to pursue."

Jamila grows quiet for a bit like she's going over what he proposed.

"I think the stuff with our exes can only affect us if we let it. And frankly, neither of us should be giving them that much power."

"That's a good point."

"So, what do we do now?"

Amari rubs his hand over Jamila's cheek and gazes into her eyes.

Fuck, she's beautiful.

He leans in and does what he's been dreaming of doing since he first met her. Their lips touch, and Amari wants to kick himself for depriving himself of this feeling for so long. Jamila clearly feels the same and wraps her arms around Amari's neck before climbing on top of him. His hands immediately go for her ass, and they both moan. Amari's dick gets harder as Jamila grinds against him. She kisses him along his jaw and down his neck as she continues to excite him thrusting her hips and rubbing her soft hands on his chest.

"Fuck, Meela," Amari whispers.

That's all he can get out. That's all his brain will allow. The feel of her against his body, her enticing scent, her touch, and her lips overwhelm his senses. He needs to be inside her. Now. Amari eases his hands into her shorts and gently glides his fingers along her wet folds. She lets out a gasp that tells him to keep going. Jamila looks up at him. Her eyes are brazen and full of need. She licks her palm and pulls his dick out. Gripping it, she slides her hand up and down.

"Ahh! Mar, don't stop." Jamila throws her head back.

Amari kisses her neck and gives her little bites as his fingertips graze her swollen nub. Jamila backs away and takes off her clothes. As much as he's enjoying her, Amari's grateful for the break in contact. He needs to get his wits about him before he busts a nut all over himself. He wants Jamila to get hers first, but by the way she's been moaning and handling his dick, that's not going to happen.

He watches carefully as she slowly makes her way back onto the bed. He takes in every curve, every tiger stripe, and every dimple along her beautiful skin. She is perfect; a feast for the senses.

She smiles, winking at him. "You likin' what you see, Mar?"

"Hell yeah."

She turns and makes that fat ass of hers clap. Unable to help himself, Amari smacks it.

"Hey! Careful, you about to leave a mark."

Amari sits up and pulls her to him. He kisses her. "I know. Why you think I did that?"

His hands are all over her. His heart is about to leap out of his chest. No woman has ever made him feel this way. He's completely vulnerable. Jamila could ask anything of him in this moment and he would give it to her. No questions asked. She must see it in his eyes because she takes his face in her hands and stares at him, her look is protective.

"I won't hurt you, Mar. I know how it feels to have your heart broken. I won't do that to you," Jamila whispers.

"I won't hurt you either," Amari replies. "I only want to take care of you."

"I'll take care of you, too."

They both have tears in their eyes. Amari stands

and removes his boxers. He picks Jamila up and gently places her in the center of the bed before climbing on top of her. They kiss again, this time with more intensity and yearning. Jamila wraps her legs around Amari's waist. His dick brushes up against her slick pussy. Amari reaches over and opens his nightstand and takes out a condom. He swallows the guilt building up as he pulls one out. This stash has been strictly reserved for the women he brings home from bars or clubs. Jamila is not just a one-and-done. He tells himself that they can now be reserved just for her. He smiles at the prospect of her being his only one. Amari rolls the condom on and pushes his dick inside of her tight, wet pussy.

"Oh, Mar," Jamila gasps.

"I know, baby. I know. You feel so good. My god, Meela."

They move in a syncopated rhythm. Slowly at first, but as Jamila meets him with each thrust, Amari moves faster.

"That's it, take all this dick," Amari praises.

"Mmmm. Mar, fuck," Jamila moans, sinking her nails into his back.

He rolls her over so he's on his back. "Ride it, Meela."

Jamila rides Amari with abandon. His eyes close tightly while he grabs her ass and digs his fingers in.

"Fuck, Meela. Go faster, baby."

Jamila does as she's told, milking Amari's dick for all it's worth. Amari matches her lifting his hips to meet her every move.

"Uh! Mar. Just like that."

"Fuck! You about to make me bust." Amari resists the urge and keeps going.

Jamila rides Amari's dick, and her beautiful breasts bounce, putting Amari in a trance.

"Shit! Mar. Oh, my god! I'm about to come."

"Go ahead, baby. Come on this dick."

"Yes! Fuck, yes. Mar!" Jamila comes and then collapses on his chest.

"What's your middle name?" she asks.

"What?" Amari asks confused.

"Your middle name, Mar. What is it?"

"Um, Isaac," he replies looking hella confused.

"Amari Isaac Hawkins, you are by far the best dick I have ever had," Jamila proudly declares.

"Why, thank you," Mar chuckles. "I was wondering where you were going with that. No woman has ever asked me that after fucking."

They both laugh. Jamila looks down. He's still hard.

"You didn't come yet."

"No, wanted to make sure you got yours first."

"Let's fix that."

Jamila slides down the bed and removes the condom. She slowly licks the veins of Amari's dick. His hands immediately go to the back of her head. She deep throats him, holding on to his ass as her head bops up and down.

"Mmmm," she moans. Slipping his dick out of her mouth, she spits on it and jerks him off.

Amari damn near falls out of bed. He grabs onto the edge of the mattress to keep himself steady. When Jamila dives back in, Amari thrusts his hips forward, fucking her mouth.

"Ugh, shit. Meela."

She sucks and slurps him up making his dick sloppier, her moans making him even harder. Women who love to suck dick are truly one of God's gifts. The way her mouth is wrapped around him makes it all too clear she's enjoying this as much as him.

She licks his balls and sucks one into her mouth, followed by the other. She spits on them and licks them more.

"God, yes. More, Meela. Fuck!" Amari moans.

Jamila jerks his dick some more. Amari's balls

tighten; he's ready to explode. Jamila opens her mouth to take his seed, and he shoots his nut in her mouth.

"Oh, goddamn."

Amari's eyes are heavy, and Jamila climbs on top of him, laying her head on his chest. He wraps his arms around her as she nuzzles her head deeper.

"I'm making you breakfast tomorrow. Anything you want," Amari announces.

Jamila giggles. "You're silly."

"That may be, but you're going to get fed real good when we wake up."

"In that case, I'll have bacon, eggs, cheesy grits, and toast."

"How you like your eggs?"

"Scrambled."

"I got you."

Jamila lets out another laugh followed by a yawn. Amari's eyelids close, and he drifts off to sleep thoroughly satisfied and more relaxed than he's felt in years.

10

JAMILA

"Enjoying your breakfast?" Amari smiles while pouring Jamila another glass of orange juice.

"Technically, this is brunch since it's almost one in the afternoon."

"Excuse me, Ms. Washington, but you would have been enjoying this meal earlier if you hadn't insisted on sleeping in."

"I wouldn't have needed to sleep in, Mr. Hawkins, if you hadn't put it on me three more times in bed and again in the shower."

"I didn't hear no complaints."

Jamila takes a bite of bacon and laughs. Amari puts down the pitcher before coming behind her to kiss the nape of her neck. His hands find her breasts, and he massages them.

"You won't be satisfied until we fuck in every room in this house, will you?" Jamila teases.

"Nope, and we got a lot of room to cover."

Jamila turns around and kisses Amari. His full lips are spellbinding. She could kiss him forever. He breaks the kiss and lifts her onto the kitchen island, slowly guiding her body to lay flat along the countertop. Jamila has on nothing but Amari's t-shirt.

He raises the shirt and looks at her pussy. "Mmm. Goddamn, woman. You stay wet."

"Only for you," Jamila purrs.

Amari looks up at her face and smiles. "I'm going to keep you wet, too."

He kneels and licks her folds.

"Fuck, Mar. Baby, that feels so good."

He buries his face between her legs and makes a meal out of her. Jamila's hands rub all over his head.

Staring up at the ceiling, all Jamila can hear is Amari as he licks, sucks, and slurps on her pussy. Her moans are drowned out by his. That is until...

"I hope ya'll don't think I'm going to clean this up when you're done," Yolanda says, announcing her arrival.

Amari looks up and wipes his mouth. "YoYo, it's Saturday, why are you here?"

"Hello to you, too, Amari."

Jamila hops off the island and attempts to straighten out her clothing.

"Sorry," Amari says. "Hello, YoYo. Why are you here?"

"Me and Peaches were at the farmer's market and the artichoke man was there, so I picked up a few for you."

"Thank you," Amari blushes.

"Hello again, Jamila." Yolanda grins, placing a hand on her hip.

"Hi, Ms. Yolanda," Jamila says, looking at the floor.

"All these bedrooms you have, and you choose to do that in here," Yolanda chides.

"Before you go judging, remind me where your youngest son was conceived," Amari begins.

"That big-mouth-ass momma of yours," Yolanda says, shaking her head, "and she wonders why I won't give her my fried chicken recipe. And you watch yourself now, youngin'. What me and my husband did at that Prince concert is nunya."

Yolanda places a tote bag with artichokes on the island, and Jamila giggles at their banter. Amari shared how Yolanda came to work for him while he made breakfast, and it only made Jamila like him even more.

Yolanda attends the same church as Vonetta. Yolanda's husband, Herb, was diagnosed with angina and their medical bills were piling up. He's a retired factory worker and in no condition to work. Yolanda is a former schoolteacher and knew she had to go back to work, but nobody wanted to hire anyone her age. Vonetta told Amari about their situation and Amari wanted to give them money outright. Yolanda was too proud to accept a handout, so she and Amari came to an agreement. She works for him Monday through Thursday as a housekeeper and he pays her a ridiculously large salary and gives her unlimited paid time off for Herb's appointments.

Jamila's tempted to ask what song Prince was performing when she and Herb were making their son, but she knows better than to say something so out-of-pocket to an elder. Especially one that just caught her getting her pussy ate.

Yolanda pokes fun at them some more before making her exit. Jamila and Amari finish their food and then head over to Vonetta's since Tennille sent a text telling them to come over right away.

Jamila opens the door and before she can greet anyone, she and Amari are ambushed by Tennille. She has an iPad in her hands and shows them the pictures from last night on Chantel Stone's Instagram. She tagged Jamila and commented:

Meet Jamila Washington y'all! I had the pleasure of getting to know her last night. This girl is going to be a star. Believe that!

Jamila is speechless. She hasn't checked her social media due to being preoccupied with other things.

Immediately, Jamila opens Instagram and finds she's basically going viral. A hundred thousand more followers on IG, and almost just as many on Twitter. The comments under Chantel's post range from recognition of her acting roles to folks who know her from the Kitten Heel. The majority are positive, aside from the unsolicited dick pics in her DMs. Jamila is ecstatic. Networking was always a part of the business, but wow! As she scrolls along Chantel's comments there's one comment that gets her attention. It's from LaWanda.

I concur with Ms. Chantel. Jamila is one to watch and if I get my way, you'll be seeing her in a certain adaptation real soon 😌*.*

Jamila shoves her screen in Amari's face. "Look!" He smiles, and gives her a huge hug, followed by Tennille and Vonetta, who Jamila just noticed are also in the room. Her phone buzzes with another IG post, this time from Kyle. It's a small snippet of Jamila singing. He comments:

Jamila, I will be in touch with your agent. You and I need to meet, there are opportunities I'd like to speak with you about.

This cannot be real. She went to a party, mingled a little, had fun entertaining the crowd, and now her life is about to change. Jamila sits on the couch trying to take everything in. Tennille's talking about all the industry folks who are all abuzz about Jamila when her phone buzzes again. It's Carly. Wow, she's been calling Jamila all day. With all the fucking she and Amari were doing, Jamila didn't think to touch her phone.

"Hi, Carly!" Jamila answers.

"Hi, Carly? Jamila Washington, you are thee *it*

girl and all you got to say is, 'Hi, Carly?' Holy hell, where have you been? Everyone is calling. They all want you. LaWanda King said she only wants you to play Kandia. You have audition after audition lined up. It's insane!"

"Holy shit!"

"Holy shit is right. You are about to blow up girl, so get ready. We're about to get paid!"

"Nice to see where your priorities are Carly," Jamila laughs.

"Hey, you knew what you were getting when you signed with me."

They talk some more and agree to meet up on Monday. Jamila ends her call with Carly and interrupts Amari and Vonetta's conversation by kissing him. When she breaks away from the kiss, he looks at her with a mix of confusion and gratitude.

"What did I do to earn that?" Amari asks.

"You took me to a party."

"Yeah, about that! How come you didn't take me?" Tennille asks.

"Stay out of this," Amari teases.

"If you hadn't taken me, I—" Jamila begins.

Amari kisses her back.

"If I hadn't taken you? Jamila, you are a star. Chantel was right about that. You would still have people knocking on your door, it just would have come at a different time."

"I'm going upstairs to pack some stuff," Jamila whispers in Amari's ear.

"Why?" he says, looking at her quizzically.

"I'm staying with you this weekend. If that's okay?" Jamila loops her arm around his and rests her chin on his shoulder.

"That's more than okay." Amari grins like he's in a trance.

Vonetta gives Jamila a congratulatory smile.

After they visit for a little while longer, Amari and Jamila head back to his place. Jamila takes her car just in case she needs it.

Jamila and Amari decide to stay in all weekend and relax. Based on the incoming messages and social media attention they're both getting, they know that starting Monday, things are going to change for both of them in more ways than one.

11

AMARI

A month has passed since LaWanda's party, and what was supposed to be just a weekend stay for Jamila turns into a whole month. The two went to Robert Emerson's screening, then the afterparty, where they were photographed by guests and paparazzi. It's been one audition after the other, and Jamila has come home from each one with a huge smile and a story of how the producer or casting director, or whoever was pleased with her performance. She recently met with Kyle and LaWanda regarding the part of Kandia. Amari, of course, was in attendance and couldn't be prouder of how Jamila handled herself during the meeting. He told her she was a total pro.

With his new responsibilities as Senior VP and

with her working at the Kitten Heel and audition-
ing, Amari and Jamila haven't had a lot of time to
spend alone or with their friends over the past few
days. They agreed to spend tonight catching up with
their friends and tomorrow night, just the two of
them.

Amari pulls into his driveway. The fellas will be
over soon to watch the fight. Kenan "The Reaper"
Matthis against Tyson "KO" Hannon, two unde-
feated champions going head-to-head in the biggest
MMA fight of the year. Amari planned on getting
tickets so they could see it live but even with all his
industry connections, there was no possible way to
do so.

When Amari enters, the smell of gumbo slaps
him in the face. He goes to the kitchen and cannot
believe his eyes. There are salmon croquettes,
chicken wings, corn fritters, and spinach patties; and
a crockpot filled with gumbo is simmering on low.
Each dish is individually wrapped in plastic on the
kitchen island.

*Did YoYo do this? If so, I have to double that woman's
salary.*

Amari helps himself to a chicken wing and corn
fritter.

Scratch that, I'm tripling it.

Right as he's about to go for a salmon croquet, Amari sees a note on the fridge.

> *I know you were planning on ordering pizza for you and your friends, but I thought this would be nicer. See you when I get home.*

That settles it, I'm marrying this woman.

He tastes the gumbo. It was truly divine. So divine, he has to convince himself not to eat the whole thing. He heads upstairs and changes out of his suit and into a pair of sweats and a t-shirt. Feeling grateful, he sends Jamila a text.

> You are unbelievable.

Two minutes later, she responds.

> Thank you.

> No. Thank you. Please believe, when you get home, I'm going to thank you properly.

> What did you have in mind?

Me getting some massage oil and rubbing it all over that incredible body of yours.

(Sigh) Yes, please.

Can't wait to see you.

Me too.

The doorbell rings and Amari heads downstairs. He's excited to spend time with his boys. Opening the door, he's shocked to find Layla on the other side.

12

JAMILA

Jamila grins at her phone as Cleo, Charmaine, and Daisy watch giggling.

"What?" Jamila asks.

"You are cheesing at that phone girl," Charmaine says.

"I know. I can't help it."

"You know, Meela. The blogs are calling you two the industry's new Black power couple," Cleo adds, taking a sip of her daiquiri.

"What blogs?" Jamila almost chokes on her Cosmo.

She and Amari have only been seen at two events, but they haven't gotten too deep into her personal life yet.

"Okay so it's only one blog, and it's Tennille's, but I'm sure there will be others ready to dub you two with that title officially," Cleo says, nudging Jamila.

Jamila takes in Cleo's words. Yes, she and Amari have, up until recently, spent a lot of time together and they clearly care for each other. Like making all that food for him and his friends. It was her way of letting him know she is serious about taking care of him. She hopes he still feels the same way about her. His ex has been more of a nuisance lately.

Ever since Layla got his cell number, she's called him almost daily, and the pics of him and Jamila only made things worse. She went from calling a couple of times a day to four or five at least. It hasn't gone unnoticed that whenever Jamila's in the room, he never answers his phone. Preferring to give her all his attention, something Jamila appreciates. Still, it would be easier to move past her uncertainty if she knew where Amari's head was. Is all this bullshit making him rethink things with her?

"This place is dead. The drinks are good but where are the hot guys?" Daisy complains.

"Amari probably has some friends, I bet they tall, dark, and handsome too," Charmaine suggests moving her hips back and forth.

"No, you guys, I don't want to crash Amari and his friends' get-together," Jamila protests.

"Crash? Girl, you practically live there. Besides, the kids are with their dad this weekend. I might find someone to take home tonight," Cleo grins.

Jamila playfully shakes her head. "Fine. Let's go."

13

AMARI

mari has never been more thankful to have Keith as a best friend. The minute he saw Layla at his door, Amari alerts Keith so he can tell the fellas to hold off on coming over until he gives the green light. It didn't take long for Amari to get a response from Keith letting him know he had his back.

Layla is seated on the couch, scanning the room. Her posture is straight as can be and exudes a haughty confidence that Amari used to find alluring but now finds annoying. He notices that nothing about her has changed. Dark brown, bone-straight tresses with a part down the middle as usual, and her makeup is minimal, with a light foundation on her tan, brown skin, gloss, and mascara. She never needed too much, just enough to enhance her natural beauty. She's dressed in a belted, ruffle wrap dress with a floral print from Badgley Mischka and medium-heeled, white Chanel sandals. Layla never left the house in sweats or jeans and always wore designer labels. If nothing has changed about her outer appearance, he doubts anything else about her has changed. Not that it even matters at this point.

"You haven't changed anything."

"The living room got repainted and I redid my office, but that's about it," Amari says dryly.

"I remember when we first saw this house. The realtor—"

"Layla, why are you here?" Amari interrupts.

"To talk about us."

"There is no us."

"I know, and that was a mistake," Layla says shakily.

Before Amari can reply, the door opens, and Jamila enters with her friends. They're all laughing and chatting until they see Amari and Layla. Immediately Amari rushes over to Jamila. After what Barry did to her, walking in on Amari alone with a strange woman would be hurtful to her even if they weren't fucking.

"Meela, I had no idea she was coming by," he

explains, taking her hands in his. He gives Jamila a pleading look, hoping she believes him. Amari has no reason to lie but given everything Meela went through, he doesn't want to risk losing her. "I asked the fellas to hold off on coming over until she was gone, and she isn't staying long."

"Okay," she says.

Jamila looks calmer than she was a second ago. Her girls on the other hand look at him with suspicion. He can't blame them; they're just looking out for her.

"Ladies, it's good to see you all again," Amari greets them, hoping to diffuse the situation.

"Hi," Cleo replies.

"Hey," Charmine says.

And Daisy simply waves.

"Do you want us to leave?" Jamila asks.

"Meela, you don't have to leave," Amari replies.

"Actually, Amari, I would prefer to talk to you alone," Layla interjects.

"Oh, would you now?" Cleo snaps.

Amari's head hangs low. This cannot be happening. If he had just called Layla back, it wouldn't be.

Jamila turns to her friends with her hand up. "Cool it, y'all."

"That's not going to happen," Amari says to

Layla. "It's good that Jamila is here. I was going to say this anyway, but she should hear it too." Amari takes a breath. "Layla, Jamila is my girlfriend…"

"I am?" She smiles.

"Baby, you live here." Amari looks at her like she must be joking.

"I know but—"

"But what? This is your home and I'm your man."

He turns back to Layla, furrowing his brow, his jaw clenched. "I am committed to my relationship with Jamila. I don't know what you thought would happen with the constant phone calls and you just stopping by, but whatever you and I had is gone."

"That's right! Go head, Mar," Charmaine cheers.

"Good answer." Daisy applauds.

Cleo and Charmaine join in applauding him as well.

"Would you three like to join my friends at the Dark Horse? It's a bar up the street. That's where they're waiting." Amari grins.

"Before we go, are they as handsome as you?" Daisy asks.

"QTNA," Cleo adds.

"They try their best," Amari chuckles.

"Good enough for me. Let's go," Charmaine says.

"When we're done here, you all can come back and join us," Amari tells them.

The ladies make their exit smiling at Amari and Jamila.

Amari takes Jamila by the hand and they join Layla who is clearly devastated. Jamila takes a seat on Amari's lap as Layla looks at them with a mix of sadness and contempt.

"I see you've settled," Layla says flatly.

"Excuse me?" Jamila snaps.

"No offense, sweetie, but you're not Mar's type. Not in the long run."

Before Jamila can reply, Layla leans in, addressing Amari.

"You seemed to have forgotten that when we first started seeing each other you had a penchant for thick girls who offered only titties and ass but being with me made you grow up. I offered you more. That's why I have been calling you, so we can work things out. You've had your fun now it's time we squash this."

"There's nothing to squash," Amari says, his tone impatient.

"Do we really have to do this with her here?" Layla turns her nose up at Jamila.

"Considering that this is her home and she's my

woman, yes, we do," Amari shoots back. "Or better yet, you can just fucking leave."

"You keep saying that like it means something. Please, Mar. Given Ms. Washington's appearance, I can only assume that you're back on your bullshit. Fucking girls with nothing but body, which could only mean one thing, you need me back in your life. That's why I'm here."

Amari burst out laughing. He laughs so hard that he clutches his stomach. When Amari finally steals a glance at Jamila, the frown she had seconds ago has melted away. Amari hooks her around her waist and pulls her closer to him. Jamila smiles at him and giggles, resting her head on his shoulder. These two women could not be more different. Jamila has on ripped jeans showing a tempting amount of skin and a tight Kitten Heel t-shirt. She's always been comfortable in her skin without having to put on airs. He can't even remember the last time he saw Layla truly relaxed. She was always on guard and ready for battle. What he once saw as raw ambition quickly became ruthlessness.

Layla was consumed with the idea of her and Amari becoming the ultimate power couple. Him climbing the ladder at Echo and her conquering the financial world working at DSQ Industries. They were on top of the world…until they weren't. And now, Amari knows what a real partnership is, making Layla's brazen attempt to get him back simply laughable.

"What the fuck are you laughing at?" Layla spits.

"You! Are you out of your fucking mind?" Still chuckling, Amari wipes away a tear.

"Amari. You're in a place where it makes sense for us to be together."

"What the hell does that even mean?" Jamila asks.

"This doesn't concern you," Layla retorts.

"The hell!" Jamila gets up and stomps over to Layla, getting in her face. "You bring your bony ass in this motherfucking house trying to claim my man, someone you threw away years ago, and what? You think I'm just going to let you? Bitch, you sound like a fucking psycho."

"And you sound like a country-ass bumpkin. Jesus, Mar, where did you even find her? What? She gave you some pussy and you decided to make her your arm candy? This is beyond pathetic."

"Stop talking to him," Jamila says sharply.

"Excuse me?"

"Amari is mine. Stop talking to him. You wanna call me a pathetic bumpkin? Sweetheart, you have no idea how pathetic you look. You've been calling him non-stop and can't seem to get the message that he don't want you. Let me guess what happened. You dropped Mar thinking you could do better, only you've found out that the grass really ain't greener."

"Not exactly," Amari replies.

Jamila and Layla turn their attention to him.

"I proposed after we were together for four years. We were both excited. Things were progressing, and I bought this house for us. We were planning our future. We were spending time with other couples. Making friends in high places. I mean, after all, that's what agreeing to marry me was really about. Isn't that right, Layla?"

Amari's anger is bubbling to the surface. He's spent years getting over what Layla did. Her betrayal nearly destroyed him. More importantly, it made him not want to deal with relationships any more. The pain she inflicted could have cost him Jamila. The thought of that angers him even more.

"Her boss is in the same fraternity as me and Keith. She introduced us and we hit it off. Soon he and I were golfing, going to ball games together, and we became friends. Layla's proximity to me made her a shoo-in for the promotion she'd been gunning for. And when she got it, we celebrated. Then shortly thereafter she started getting distant. I thought she was cheating until I found out that she had been using her relationship with me as leverage at her job. Once I served my purpose, she no longer needed me, so she left."

Jamila looks at Layla with fury in her eyes. "You evil, heartless ass bitch! You get the fuck out our house right now!"

"Your house! Bitch, I helped him pick this house!" Layla shouts.

Tears stream down Layla's face and she rushes over to Amari and takes his hands in hers.

"Mar, I'm sorry. Baby, I thought that climbing the ladder would get me everything I needed but I was wrong. I love my job, but I miss you. You, Mar. You were the one, but I was too foolish to see it. Back then, you were just a means to an end for me. I'm sorry. I realize that I shouldn't have hurt you. I realize that I love you. I always have. Please give us another chance. Please!"

Amari snatches his hands away. "No. After all that bullshit you put me through. Let me make this clear. I love Jamila. I don't want anything to do with you. Now leave."

"Mar..."

"Layla, leave!" Amari yells.

Defeated, Layla looks at him with pity. She turns to Jamila.

"He's a good one. Don't make the same mistake I did." And with that, Layla leaves.

Amari shakes his head, unable to believe what the fuck just happened. The really fucked up part is, had Layla done this not long after she left, he would have taken her back. He frowns at the thought. Slowly, Jamila walks over and stands by his side. She runs her fingernails over his scalp. He closes his eyes and leans his head back, and her lips press against his. He slowly opens his eyes to see her looking at him lovingly.

"I am so sorry you had to deal with that," she says.

"You're sorry? Meela, I should be apologizing to you. If I had just taken one of her calls, I could have avoided this mess."

"I get it, though. You didn't want to talk to her, and given what she did, why the fuck would you?"

"I guess." Amari looks away with a contemplative expression.

Jamila nudges him. "Hey."

He looks back up at her.

"You got closure, that's all that matters. She needed to realize that her mistake couldn't be undone, and you deserved an apology. Shiiitt, that's more than I got."

They laugh.

"Look if you don't want anyone over after all that, I'm sure your friends will understand. I know mine will," Jamila offers.

"No, it's cool. They can come through. I'm not letting her ruin my night."

"Good."

They text their friends, letting them know to come. Minutes later, the doorbell rings. Amari opens it to find his homey Tyrone with his arm around Cleo, while his friend Victor is chatting with Daisy, and his boy Daeshon comes in walking hand-in-hand with Charmaine. Keith is the only one stag.

"Shit, if I had known it was going to be this type of party, I would have brought Erika."

"Tell her to come over. We got plenty of food, thanks to this one." Amari hooks his thumb at Jamila.

"It's alright. She's visiting with her mom anyway."

Jamila reheats the appetizers and makes sure the gumbo is ready. Amari grabs plates, bowls, glasses, and utensils, and they spread everything out. While everybody descends on the food, Amari goes to grab the rum punch.

"Did you mean what you said?" Jamila asks.

"I meant everything."

"You know which part I meant, Mar."

Amari puts the pitcher down and wraps his arms around Jamila's waist, pulling her to him. He looks her in the eyes, his stance unwavering.

"I love you, Jamila."

She smiles, holding his face in her hands. "I love you, too, Amari."

14

———

AMARI

The Hawkins family enters the Kitten Heel. Amari and Tennille watch as Vonetta looks at the décor.

"It looks just like 'Moulin Rouge,'" Vonetta says, smiling.

"That's what I thought when I first came here," Amari agrees.

Amari turns to Kenya to get her opinion but she's too busy staring at Ramone.

"Welcome to the Kitten Heel," Ramone says smirking.

"Thank you. It's my first time here," Kenya replies.

"Hopefully it won't be your last," he says, winking which causes Kenya to blush.

Amari looks at Tennille with a teasing grin. "Looks like Ramone might be your new stepdaddy."

"That would be nice but considering that all she does is go to work then home, I wouldn't count on it. It was a miracle we got her to come here," Tennille replies. Her tone has a hint of sadness.

"You okay, T?"

"Yeah, it's just that Dad and Shelley got engaged last week and he's been posting non-stop on social media. I think mom's upset, but she won't say anything."

"Shit."

Amari's not surprised. Kenya tends to keep her feelings close to her chest. When things ended between her and Emil, she didn't tell anyone for months.

"I'll check in with her, make sure she's okay," Amari says.

"Thanks, Uncle Pooh."

"Of course," Amari says, hugging Tennille.

They take their seats at a specially reserved table. Amari looks around, and to no surprise, the place is packed. Jamila certainly draws a crowd. Her admirer, Frank, is back. He's wearing a nice suit and he has a huge bouquet of roses––he's ready to shoot his shot again. Amari hopes he reconsiders. He'd hate to have to embarrass Frank in front of all these people, but he definitely will.

Cleo takes the stage. "Good evening, everyone, and welcome to the Kitten Heel. I'm your gracious host and bartender extraordinaire, Cleo!"

Everyone applauds and cheers.

"Thank you, thank you." Cleo blows a kiss to the audience.

"As always, we have an amazing show for you tonight. Starting us off is the incomparable Ms. Jamila Washington with a special performance dedicated to a certain somebody."

Cleo winks at Amari. Frank lets out a loud cheer.

I know this nigga don't think she's talking about him.

Cleo continues her intro. "So, relax, have a drink, and enjoy the show."

The crowd applauds and cheers again, this time even louder.

Jamila comes out to the opening of "Whatever Lola Wants" from the musical *Damn Yankees*. She has on a tight red number that reminds Amari of the dresses En Vogue wore in the video for "Giving Him Something He Can Feel." She sings the tune, staring directly at Amari, and he's immediately hypnotized.

Amari never thought he would feel this way ever again. What started as a ruse to get Mrs. Gordon off his back has turned into something he can't be without. So, yes, Jamila has his whole heart and soul. She has his love, his patience, and his protection. She has all of him, and he never plans to take any of it away.

Moving her hips seductively, Jamila makes her way off the stage toward Amari. She gets closer to him as she repeats the line telling him to give in. She slowly slides her body over his. They're now face-to-face. Their lips are only inches apart. Amari aches with need. He has to kiss her. Just as he leans in, Jamila teases him by leaning back. He frowns as she smirks. She turns so she's perched on his lap as she finishes the song, her ass right on his erection.

When the song ends, thunderous applause erupts. Amari wraps his arms around Jamila's waist. Unfortunately, she doesn't stay there for long.

Frank comes over with his bouquet. He takes Jamila's hand, pulling her into his arms. Amari stands up ready to check him.

"Get your motherfucking hands off her!" Amari barks.

Before Frank can respond Amari has him hemmed up by his collar. Jamila gives Amari a look that tells him she'll handle it. Amari lets go of Frank but stays close, just in case.

"That's the type of nigga you're fucking with?" Frank asks straightening out his clothes.

"Yes, I am," Amari bites back.

"Alright Frank, what do you want?" Jamila asks impatiently.

"Jamila, you're incredible! Run away with me!" Frank exclaims.

"Frank, we've been over this before. I'm not running away with you. You. Are. Married."

"I left my wife."

"What!" Jamila yells.

Frank gets on his knee and pulls out a ring. Amari, Jamila, Tennille, Kenya, and Vonetta all look at him like he's lost his goddamn mind.

"Jamila, will you marry me?"

"No, fool," Jamila says. "Frank, we are not, nor will we ever be a thing. I'm with Amari, and even if I wasn't, you and I would never happen."

"Yeah, but that was because of my wife."

"No, it was because you never had a shot."

"Seriously? Even with all the money I threw on stage and the flowers and shit?"

"Still, no shot."

"And even with me offering to take you on trips?"

"No, Frank." Jamila rolls her eyes.

"So even when I...?"

"No, nigga. Damn!" Amari says, exasperated. "Take a motherfucking hint and take your dumb ass back to your wife."

"Who just had a baby," Jamila adds.

"No, he was not trying to flirt with you while his wife is at home with a newborn," Vonetta chimes in.

"Yes, he was, Ms. Vonetta."

"Boy, if you don't take your trifling ass back home. Your poor wife is dealing with a new baby, and you're at a bar trying to pick up women!" Kenya gets in Frank's face.

"Yo' ass better go on, Frank. You don't want me to let my sister come after you. It'll be a million times worse than anything I could do," Amari states plainly.

Frank looks at Kenya who actually growls and gets the fuck on. As he heads for the door, Kenya yells at him.

"I hope your wife beats your ass and your prostate falls out!" Kenya yells.

The crowd cheers for Kenya who smiles and gives a bow. Ramone approaches her.

"I'm impressed." He smiles.

"And where were you during all of this?" Kenya says with fake bravado.

"Manning the door. Besides, Jamila knows how to handle Frank, and apparently so do you."

"It was nothing." Kenya shrugs.

"It didn't look like nothing," Ramone smiles.

"Ramone, this is Kenya. Kenya this is Ramone," Jamila introduces them grinning.

"Nice to meet you, Kenya."

"You, too."

"You are a big man, aren't you?" Vonetta smiles. "You know my Kenya is single."

"Momma!" Kenya looks beyond embarrassed.

"What? I got your brother a woman, now it's your turn."

"I am so sorry," Kenya says.

"It's okay. I need to go back to the door. You all enjoy the rest of the show." Ramone struts back to the entrance.

"Momma, I think you scared him off," Amari smiles teasingly.

"Oh, nonsense. We'll invite him over to the house for dinner."

"Oh, god," Kenya groans, covering her face.

Amari and Jamila laugh as Tennille comforts her mother, trying to hide her laughter.

"Kenya, girl, stop fussing. Look at them. I obviously have great instincts about these things."

Vonetta turns her attention to Amari and Jamila who are cuddled up. "Hey, lovebirds, aren't you two happy I lied to Mrs. Gordon?"

"Yes, Momma."

"Yes, Ms. Vonetta."

Amari and Jamila reply at the same time in a 'how many times are you going to mention this?' tone.

"Don't go getting flippant, or I'll tell her that y'all broke up."

They know she's bluffing but don't want to risk it.

"Yes ma'am," they reply together again.

It's a little after seven on Wednesday when Amari finally gets home. Today was another long day at the office, and he is beyond tired. The producer of *Sioux* is getting pushback from the local government about the permits for the shooting location, which led to a lengthy discussion that included Amari and Echo's legal team along with the mayor, Grady Turner. It basically boiled down to Mayor Turner wanting more money from Echo, citing that filming would inconvenience the local economy, which was a load of bullshit. Tourism has gone up fifty-eight percent in that little town since filming started. Something that Amari had to remind him of. He also had to remind him they could nullify their contract and film elsewhere if need be. Once the legal team concurred, mentioning the clause in the contract, Mayor Turner became a lot more understanding.

Amari parks his car in the driveway and waves to a neighbor. He's looking forward to having a nice meal with Jamila and the two of them relaxing for the rest of the night. He had Bree make reservations at The Szechuan Garden for Friday. Amari wants to take her out on a fancy date. With all the attention they've been getting since LaWanda's party, both have opted to stay at home most nights. Szechuan Garden is the perfect choice. Jamila loves Chinese food, and this is one of the best joints in the city. It's rated five stars by every food critic nationwide, has a Michelin star, and the head chef is a James Beard award winner. Amari knows they'll have an amazing time.

When he opens the front door, he's surprised to find Jamila dressed in a black pin-striped pencil skirt that stops at her heavenly thighs. She's coupled it with a white collared, button-down blouse. Her hair is in a messy bun on top of her head, and she's wearing black thick-rimmed glasses. She looks like a sexy secretary. Seconds––mere seconds––is all it takes for Amari to get a second wind along with a stiff erection.

"Good evening, Meela."

"Good evening, Mr. Hawkins. If you'll come with me to your office, we have lots of work to do."

"Do we?"

"Yes, I have a lot of DICK-tation to take."

"That's good because I have a lot to give you."

"Oh, I'm well aware, sir."

Amari heads for his bedroom.

"Where are you going?" Jamila asks.

"To get condoms."

Jamila pulls out some condoms from her skirt pocket and unfurls them with a wicked smile spreading across her lips.

"Nice job, Ms. Washington."

"That's why you hired me."

Amari follows Jamila into his home office and proceeds to bend her over his desk and lift her skirt. She has on garters and stockings but no panties.

"Goddamn Meela," Amari mutters.

He rubs her ass and gives it a smack, and she responds by wiggling it for him. Amari gets on his knees and licks her ass cheeks one at a time.

"Mmmm. That feels good, Mr. Hawkins," Jamila moans, clenching the edge of his desk.

"Glad you approve."

Amari takes a bite of each cheek.

Jamila widens her legs and Amari sticks his tongue between them.

"Ahh. Mar, please."

Amari sucks on her swollen nub making Jamila's legs shake.

"Oh, fuck, fuck," Jamila moans as she wets Amari's mouth.

Amari licks his lips and stands. Jamila is damn near on the floor; probably because her legs are so weak from his tonguing. After knocking the papers off his desk, Amari lifts Jamila and lays her on her back, scooting her to the edge. He grabs a condom and sheaths himself before pushing his dick inside of her.

"Oh, shit," Amari screams.

He moves faster with each thrust, knowing that's how Jamila likes it, but Amari's not sure how long he can last. This is beyond heaven, bliss, and perfection. None of those words sum up how good Jamila's pussy is. The feeling is incomprehensible. No one is better than her, and her taste is beyond compare. She's like nothing he's had on his tongue before.

And it's not just the sex—it's her. She's everything he's ever wanted and more. A hot, relaxing bath, followed by a good meal and a warm, soft bed during a cold winter's night would feel like solitary confinement compared to being in her presence.

"Shit, Mar. I'm coming." Jamila screams as her fingers dig into his arms.

"Me too. Fuck, Meela! Oh, shit. I can't...I can't sttttooppp."

Amari comes harder and longer than he ever has before. When he finishes, he collapses on top of Jamila.

"That was just what I needed," Amari pants.

"You sounded stressed when I called you earlier, so I wanted to surprise you."

"I appreciate it."

"You want to take me upstairs?" Jamila asks.

Amari replies by standing up to take her by the waist and lifting her. She wraps her legs around him as he carries her upstairs, giggling the whole way up.

JAMILA

It's Friday night, and Amari and Jamila are ready for a night on the town. Amari first surprised her by having his assistant Bree sneakily get Jamila's measurements and use his credit card to get her a designer couture gown from Mtindo, a Black-owned boutique. The dress is a curve-hugging, emerald green, lace bodice gown with enchanting sparkle accents and a dipped back. Jamila feels like a million, no, a billion bucks. Her hair is styled in an elegant updo, and her makeup is flawless. That was Amari's second surprise; having Charmaine and Cleo glam her up for the night. Cleo did her hair, and Charmaine did her makeup. Now, Jamila stands before him, and Amari looks utterly speechless.

"You like what you see?" Jamila teases.

"I love what I see."

"Be careful, Mr. Hawkins. Don't go messing up all our hard work," Cleo says.

"I wouldn't dream of it. You ladies did your thing. We will definitely have y'all on hand to get Meela ready come award season."

Jamila giggles. "I wouldn't go that far, Amari."

"Why not? I would," he smirks.

The amount of confidence this man has in Jamila never ceases to astound her. They make goo-goo eyes for a while before Charmaine cuts in.

"Y'all are going to be late. Looking at each other like you're going to fuck right in front of us."

Amari and Jamila laugh. She's not far off.

"We should head out," Charmaine says, carefully hugging Jamila.

Jamila hugs them back before they head for the door. Cleo turns back and looks at Amari.

"Keep taking care of our girl," she says.

Amari smiles. "I'm on it." Cleo and Charmaine give him warm smiles before leaving.

Minutes later, Amari and Jamila are in the car on their way to dinner.

"I didn't get a chance to tell you how dapper you look, darling," Jamila flirts.

"Thank you, baby," Amari smirks. "You be careful with how you look at me. I'ma have to pull over and lift that dress up."

"Handle your business, Mr. Hawkins."

"Don't tempt me," Amari says as he bites his lip. "But seriously, this place is a known spot for famous folks to turn up, so there'll be paparazzi, and if they get a snap of you, I want you looking fly. With all the buzz you've been getting online, they will definitely want to take pics."

Amari's not wrong. Between the parties and the recent TV appearances, Jamila has racked up more attention these past few weeks than ever before. Auditions for Kandia are starting soon. While LaWanda and Kyle are going to bat for Jamila with the executives of Echo, Carly, the angel she is, provided insight on how the executives are reluctant to go with an unknown actor. To his credit, Amari has remained neutral. He doesn't discuss anything in great detail at home when Jamila asks about his day. LaWanda, however, has told Jamila how Amari has disclosed his relationship with her to everyone involved in the project. While singing her praises wildly, Amari made sure to make the executives aware of his opinion on how she'd do in the role.

"I will be getting in that pussy and folding you

up when we get home though. Believe that," Amari confidently declares. Jamila chuckles as Amari winks at her.

They arrive at the restaurant and Amari hands the valet his keys and a hundred-dollar bill. Everyone in L.A. knows, if you tip the valets well, your car will come back the way you gave it to them.

When Amari and Jamila enter the restaurant, it's like time has stopped. All eyes are on them, and a few actors, writers, and producers come over to say hi. Once they're seated, Jamila orders an appletini while Amari opts for a sloe gin fizz.

"That's a unique choice," Jamila comments.

"I'm a unique man. Now, if you'll excuse me, I'm going to head to the men's room, be right back." Amari takes her hand and kisses her knuckles.

Jamila smiles and kisses his hand right back. Settling into her seat, Jamila sips her water and reflects on where her life is to date. She has a good man--scratch that--a great man, and she's making moves in her career. Jamila's dreams are coming true. She closes her eyes and lets out a relaxing sigh when she hears a familiar voice.

"Jamila, is that you?"

Her muscles tense immediately. She'd know that voice from anywhere.

Barry.

Her mood immediately sours.

"It is you. I thought so," Barry says, grinning like an idiot.

"Yes, Barry. It's me. We dated and lived together for years. You shouldn't have that much trouble recognizing me."

"Right." Barry clears his throat. "Well, I just wanted to come over and congratulate you on every-thing. I've been seeing you all over IG. I always knew you'd make it."

"Are you fucking kidding me?" Jamila spits.

The waitress approaches and gives Jamila a look silently asking if she's okay. Jamila smiles and nods at her. She delivers their drinks and then quickly scurries away.

"Meela..." Barry starts.

"No, you cheated on me and then kicked me out all because you didn't believe in me."

"That was something I deeply regret. I should have been more considerate and sensitive."

"That's all well and good, Barry, but where was all this concern when I was sleeping on Charmaine's lumpy couch? It's funny how now that I'm moving up in the industry, you're sorry."

They simply stare at each other. Jamila wants to

do nothing more than punch Barry in the face. Meanwhile, he looks like he wants to fall to his knees and beg her forgiveness.

When Amari returns, he scans Jamila's face, and there's clearly tension in the air, so she doesn't bother trying to hide it.

"Hello," Amari says to Barry as he takes his seat. "Are you a friend of Meela's?"

It's obvious she and Barry are not friends, but Amari's the type to step in and try to defuse a situation, and Jamila loves that about him.

"Barry, this is my boyfriend, Amari Hawkins," Jamila says.

The minute Amari hears Barry's name, Jamila feels his energy become protective.

"Wait, you're *the* Amari Hawkins. The Senior VP of Programming at Echo?" Barry says.

Barry sounds like he's in the presence of God.

Wow! All that regret sure went out the window quickly.

"Yeah, man. That's me," Amari says flatly.

"Oh, my God!" Barry's excitement is beyond embarrassing. "Do you mind if we chat for a bit?"

"Listen, man. Meela and I are having a date night and—"

"Oh, it's fine. Meela doesn't mind and I'll be quick," Barry interjects.

Jamila looks at Barry like he's lost his goddamn mind. Clearly, Barry isn't reading the room because he proceeds to take a seat at their table.

"This is incredible to meet you. I don't know if Meela told you but I'm a screenwriter. I would love to have a meeting with you about my latest script."

"I don't look at unsolicited material," Amari replies.

"I understand that but you're going to want to read this one. It's like nothing you've ever read before."

"Is that right?" Amari says. His tone is filled with mockery.

"It is. Let me give you the pitch..."

"That's really not necessary. I'm aware of your work."

"You are?" Barry says with stars in his eyes.

"You are?" Jamila says with confusion.

"Yeah, baby. You see when you told me about Mr. Barry, here, I did a little digging."

Jamila sees the mischievous look in Amari's eyes and knows it's about to go down.

"Go ahead, babe," she says.

Amari's eyes never leave Barry. "Do you

remember when you told Jamila that your boss was going to read one of your scripts?"

Barry lets out a cough and looks down. "I should go. I don't want to disturb your evening."

"You've already done that," Amari says sharply. "Do you want to tell Meela what happened, or should I?"

Barry doesn't look up or say anything.

"Very well. Barry's boss, Grant Carter, is a good friend of mine. He read Barry's script and realized it sounded eerily similar to one that a client of his wrote. Turns out Barry read the script first, wrote his own version, and he's been fired from the agency. Did I get all that right, Bare?"

"It was, um, nice meeting you. Bye Meela." Barry stands and quickly leaves the restaurant.

The waitress returns. "Oh, good. You got rid of him."

"I'm sorry?" Jamila says.

"The loser who was at your table. Word around town is that he's been going to every restaurant frequented by industry people the past couple of weeks trying to get them to read his script. So pathetic." The waitress shakes her head.

Jamila bursts out laughing as does Amari.

The waitress smiles. "What's so funny?"

"He's my ex!" Jamila laughs some more.

"Holy crap. Seriously? Wow, well congrats. You've certainly come up." The waitress sends a friendly smile Amari's way.

She leans over the table and plants kisses on his lips. "Yes, I have."

16

JAMILA

It's been two weeks since the audition for *Just an Ordinary Girl,* and Jamila still hasn't heard anything. If it wasn't for Amari and her steady TV gigs, she'd be in a serious funk. While she is disappointed that it's taking so long, she understands. This book is important, and the film adaptation is going to be huge. Echo would be foolish to rush the process when so many people are looking forward to seeing what Kyle and company come up with.

Jamila Facetimes her mom. It's been so long since she's actually seen her, so talking to her is a much-needed distraction. She also misses her something fierce.

"We're going to be coming out to L.A. next week, baby girl!" Etta Mae sings happily.

Jamila grins at her mother's wonderful news. She can't wait to see her folks and properly introduce them to Amari. He's spoken to Etta Mae a couple of times, and she found him absolutely charming. On the other hand, her father, Clem, has been less than receptive when it comes to speaking to Amari. He's not too pleased that they live together. Jamila officially moved in the day after Layla's surprise visit. He's even turning one of the guest rooms into her own quiet space for her to rehearse and relax. He really is something special.

Jamila smiles as she thinks about the auditions, the meetings with Carly, and the events Amari took her to. She can't wait to see her parents so they can see firsthand why she loves L.A. so much.

Clem takes the iPad from Etta Mae.

"What's this I hear about you working at a strip club, Meela?"

"Daddy, I don't work at a strip club. It's a cabaret."

"Uh huh. I don't know what that is. You wasn't taking off your clothes were you?"

"No, Daddy. And who even told you about the Kitten Heel?"

"Barry. He moved back home a few days ago. Living with his parents. Suppose to start working for his pops at the car wash."

It took all Jamila's willpower not to start laughing. That's what his cheating, thieving ass gets. The entertainment industry is a small world, and it didn't take long before Barry's name was mud after what he tried to pull.

"What are you doing talking to him anyway?"

"Look, baby, you know me. I was ready to bust that little fucker's head open 'til he started talking about you being naked on stage," Clem replies.

"You have nothing to worry about, I'm not naked." *Well, not entirely, but I'm not telling you that.* "Feel free to bust his head all you want."

"Will do, pumpkin. Now speaking of young men I don't approve of, I think it's about time I speak with this man you living with. What's his name? Omar?"

"Amari, Daddy."

"Clem, don't you act out. You be nice to Amari. He's a good man," Etta Mae interjects.

"Yeah, yeah. I'll be good, baby. Just want to make sure he's treating our pumpkin right," Clem says, kissing Etta Mae on the cheek.

Jamila smiles. Her parents' relationship has always been the prototype for how a partnership should be. Her dad is traditional but not so stuck in his ways that he doesn't listen to or respect her mother. Clem makes the money while Etta Mae runs the house.

"Go on and tell him I'd like to chat, Meela," Clem says.

"Okay." Jamila takes the iPad and heads to Amari's office and gently knocks on the door.

"Come on in, baby," he calls out.

When Jamila enters, a smile spreads across Amari's face. It has only been thirty minutes since he's last seen her at breakfast, but he's taking her in like he hasn't seen her in years. Jamila can't help but smile back.

God, I love this man.

AMARI

Damn, I love this woman.

Amari's smile still hasn't left his face. As Jamila bounces into his office, he notices she's holding an iPad. She probably wants to show him another vacation destination she found. She suggested a trip somewhere after she finds out whether or not she gets cast. It will either be a celebratory vacation or a pity party—her words–. No matter what, Amari knows he wants to be right by her side. Ever since Jamila told him she has never been out of the U.S., it became something Amari wanted to remedy quickly. Having been to Europe, parts of Asia, and the Caribbean himself, Amari wants to show her the world. Take her to all his favorite places so she can experience what he loves for herself.

"How can I help you?" Amari smirks.

"My dad wants to talk to you," Jamila says turning the iPad so he can see her parents.

Oh, shit! A wave of relief passes over Amari. He was two seconds from saying something that would have gotten him even higher on Mr. Washington's shit list.

"Hello, Mr. and Mrs. Washington."

"Hi, Amari," Etta Mae smiles.

"Hey," Clem says flatly. Etta Mae nudges him with her elbow. "Look, son, I want to talk to you about your intentions with my daughter."

"Okay, sir. Well, my intentions with Jamila are clear. I want to take care of her."

"Meela doesn't need a man to take care of her. She's capable of doing that on her own," Clem says sternly.

"I meant no disrespect, sir. I am aware of how resilient and strong Meela is. That's simply the dynamic of our relationship. Meela takes care of me and I, in turn, look after her. We love each other, and I know we got together rather quickly, but I assure you that Jamila is in safe and loving hands being with me."

"Mmmhmm. How do I know that for sure? Barry was supposed to be there for her, and look how that turned out."

Amari is filled with conviction. He makes sure to look directly into the camera when he responds, "Barry was a boy pretending to be a man. I am a man. I have done nothing but look out for Jamila's best interest from the moment we became close, and I intend to continue doing so for as long as she'll let me."

"Is that right?" Mr. Washington grins, but Amari can tell he's not quite convinced.

"That is right, sir. As a matter of fact, if I ever do wrong by your daughter, you can shoot me in the foot."

"Mar, are you nuts? He'll actually do it, you know." Jamila's eyes are wide with shock.

"She's not lying, Amari. He will do it," Etta Mae adds.

"I am serious. If I ever hurt Jamila, Mr. Washington can shoot me. That's how confident I am that it won't happen."

"Aw, that's so romantic and also a little fucked up," Jamila chuckles.

"Watch your language, Meela," Etta Mae says.

"Sorry, Momma."

Amari smirks at her. Jamila pokes out her tongue.

"Is his answer good enough for you, Daddy?"

"I guess. We'll see if he passes muster when we get out there and meet face-to-face."

"I look forward to it, sir," Amari grins.

"Yeah, I'm sure you do. Give the iPad back to my princess."

Amari hands the iPad back to Jamila. She says her goodbyes, and as soon as they end the call Jamila gives Amari a long passionate kiss.

"Wow, what was that for?" he says, squeezing her waist.

"That was to remember me by because once you meet my dad, you might not want to bother with me. He's never met a boyfriend this early into the relationship."

"I think I handled myself pretty well."

"You did, but that's the problem. Now that he sees that you aren't scared of him, he's going to ramp it up."

"Let him. I'm not going anywhere."

18

JAMILA

Jamila is pleased to see her mother so excited. Etta Mae talks the tour guide's ear off. The minute they got off the plane, her mom asked about all the touristy things she and her dad could do in L.A. Even though Jamila has been here for three years, this is her parents' first visit. They run a ranch-style B&B in town and can rarely get away.

"So, that's really The Rock's house?" Etta Mae asks.

"Yep, it sure is. And if you look on your left, you'll see two-time Oscar winner Denzel Washington's house," the tour guide says.

"Oh, my god! Clem, take a picture!"

"Why? All you can see is a large gate, can't even see the house."

"I don't care. Take it anyway," Etta Mae demands.

Amari wraps his arm around Jamila's waist. "That's going to be us in a few years," he whispers.

Jamila gives him a funny look. "That's us now. I'm always getting you to do what I want."

"True, and I have no intention of ever saying no to you." Amari smiles.

Jamila leans in and gives him a sweet kiss on the lips.

"Alright, that's enough you two," Clem says.

"Oh, Clem. Leave them be." Etta Mae looks at Jamila and smiles. "We got a huge star in our midst. She'll need Amari to look after her as she gains more fans."

"Momma." Jamila blushes.

A couple of people on the tour recognized Jamila from her Bear Burger commercial and the pics from the Robert Emmerson party. Even though it was a private event, pictures of her and Amari's arrival were leaked and went viral. The tour patrons took pictures with Jamila and asked her about some of the celebrities she's met.

"What? You already have fans. Your star is only

going to get bigger baby," Etta Mae exclaims, grinning proudly.

"She's right, Meela," Amari says. "You're meant to do great things. And I'll be right there every step of the way."

"Until you aren't," Clem mutters.

Etta Mae shoots him a scathing look that tells him to keep it zipped. Jamila snuggles close to Amari and squeezes his hand, silently telling him not to listen to her father. He hears her message loud and clear and kisses her temple. Though Jamila loves and respects her father, he's making her want this visit to be over a lot sooner. She knew he would be hard on Amari, but he is outright disrespecting him. Jamila is beyond disappointed. She was looking forward to seeing her parents, and now her dad is ruining it. It all started this morning when they flew in. Amari made sure Bree had a car waiting for them at the curb of the airport when they arrived. He also made sure they flew first class and had a room at the five-star Park-Barrington Hotel in Beverly Hills. All Clem could do was complain about the "uppity" accommodations. And it's only gotten worse as the day wears on.

After they finished the tour, they visited the Hollywood sign, the Hollywood Walk of Fame, and

TCL Chinese Theater, had lunch at the Roscoe's on Gower, and then took the celebrity bus tour. Etta Mae has a whole itinerary planned for the weekend including Universal Studios, Venice Beach, and Leimert Park. Jamila prays Etta Mae can get Clem in much better spirits by the time they go to dinner tonight. Hopefully, the nap they plan to take will help.

19

——————

AMARI

The nap didn't help. Jamila told Amari that her dad would chill once he got some rest, but that did not happen. When they picked up her parents for dinner, Clem kept grumbling about not needing special treatment or a fancy car. He then went on to complain about everything, from the high gas prices to the population. The man literally complained that there were too many people in Los Angeles.

The dinner itself isn't going any better. They went to a high-end steak house, and the trip from Beverly Hills to Malibu took a little over an hour.

"I don't understand why we had to drive all the way here just to have a steak," Clem says.

This man is a pain. It's understandable not to like certain things, but Clem has something negative to say about everything, and now he wants to complain about a steakhouse, of all things. Though Amari loves Jamila he's counting the days until her parents leave. The truly fucked up part is he's enjoying getting to know Etta Mae—she's an absolute sweetheart; it's Clem who he really wants gone. Maybe on the next visit, she can come by herself.

"Daddy, this is one of the best restaurants in LA," Jamila explained.

"There aren't any good ones by the hotel?" Clem asked.

"There are plenty, sir, but Jamila mentioned how much you enjoy a good steak, and I thought this would be a nice choice. We got a table by the window with a beautiful view," Amari replied.

"Pffft! A lot of good that did, it'll be dark soon. Then we won't be able to see shit," Clem grumbles.

"Clem! Behave yourself," Etta Mae warns. "I'm sorry. This is a lovely choice, Amari."

"Thank you."

Things simmer down when dinner is served. Clem even has to admit that his ribeye is cooked perfectly, but the minute the check arrived, the shit storm starts up again.

Amari reaches for the check at the same time as Clem.

"Mr. Washington, I insist on paying. You and Mrs. Washington are guests."

"Guests? Boy, we're here to visit our daughter, and that means paying for her meal. If you want to pay for yours, then that's fine."

"Good lord, Clem. Let the man pay," Etta Mae says, annoyance seeming to lace her tone.

"Etta, let me handle this. Listen to me, boy—"

"I'm going to need you to stop referring to me as a boy. I already explained I'm a man," Amari says making direct eye contact with Clem.

"I suppose you think you're a man 'cause you got money, a fancy car, and them expensive suits?"

"No, sir. I'm a man without all that stuff. I've shown you and Mrs. Washington nothing but respect, I'd just like to be shown the same in return."

"Respect? You call moving our daughter into your house like you own her being respectful?"

"Sir, Jamila chose to move in with me, and that was only after things became serious between us."

"After what happened with Barry, Jamila jumping at the chance to live with another man isn't what she needed. She could have come home," Clem snaps.

"Daddy, that wasn't an option," Jamila argues.

"Why? You could have come back to Nebraska and saved up some money, then tried acting again in a few years."

"That's what this is about, isn't it? You never wanted me to leave. Daddy, this is my dream, and now things are finally starting to happen. All my hard work is paying off. And I have a wonderful man to share it with. Why can't you be happy for me?"

"I am happy for you, baby. It's just hard knowing that your only child is thousands of miles away and living with some rich guy you don't know shit about," Clem says that last part while looking right at Amari.

"Once you both meet my family this Saturday, you'll see that I'm not some rich guy who stole your daughter."

At least I hope so.

Vonetta insisted on having a small gathering at the house for Etta Mae and Clem while they are in town so the families could meet in person. Iman and Zuri are even going to join in on FaceTime.

"I can't wait. I just know it's going to be lovely," Etta Mae gushes.

"Fine, whatever," Clem grunts.

Amari takes care of the check, the drive back to the hotel is quicker than the drive to the restaurant, thank God.

20

JAMILA

The next morning, Jamila picks up her parents and they enjoy a nice breakfast at the hotel restaurant. Things are going nicely. Her dad even promises to be nicer to Amari. Just as they're heading to Griffith Park, Jamila's phone buzzes. It's Daisy.

"Hey Daisy, I'm driving so you're on speaker!" Jamila says immediately.

"Hey Meela," Daisy greets her.

Daisy's background is so loud, it sounds like she's at Coachella or something. "What's all that noise? Are you having a party and didn't invite me?"

"Never! The Kitten Heel brunch crowd is a lively bunch, darling."

"Right, I forgot that started today."

Ms. Liz decided to try her hand at having afternoon cabaret performances with a brunch theme. Since the Kitten Heel has a full kitchen, opening earlier and serving food and drinks would be an easy addition. It was kind of a no-brainer. Besides, who in L.A. doesn't do brunch?

"Yeah, so why aren't you here for the inaugural celebration?"

"Remember my parents are in town. I'll be back to work next week."

"Oh my god, you should bring them!"

"No can do, we're headed to Griffith Park."

"Booo! Don't take them to the tourist traps, take them someplace fun."

"I wouldn't mind seeing where you work, sweetie," Etta Mae chimes in.

"But, Momma, you had all these places you wanted to see." Jamila tries to steer the conversation away from the Kitten Heel. "Besides, we're almost there."

"Not according to Google Maps. It says we have a ways to go. And if you ain't doing nothing to be ashamed of, you shouldn't have a problem showing your momma and me where you work," Clem argues.

"Okay. Let's go. I'll see you in a bit, Daisy."

"Yay!"

Before arriving, Jamila texts Cleo. She asks her to hide the picture of Jamila in her Josephine Baker costume hanging by the bar. She never gets a response, so who knows if Cleo even read her text.

Jamila's heart is racing, and she keeps telling herself they'll just pop in, say hi, and leave, but she knows better. Her mom is a social butterfly and will try to talk to everyone Jamila works with.

When they enter, Etta Mae looks around at the décor. "Look, Clem! It's like we're in Paris," she says, filled with excitement.

Clem, on the other hand, has his eyes fixed somewhere else. Jamila follows her father's gaze. It's officially confirmed—Cleo didn't get her text.

Shit.

Clem looks back at Jamila with a mix of anger and shock. "Jamila Cheyenne Washington, is that you?" Clem points to the picture.

Daisy chooses this moment to appear. "Meela, you're here! And this must be your parents."

"Daisy, I'll check in with you later." Jamila looks at her like, *quickly, save yourself.*

"Uh, is everything okay?"

"No really, Daisy. I'll talk to you later."

"Oh, okay."

"Jamila, answer me," Clem says.

"Come with me." Jamila escorts her parents to the dressing room.

She peeks in first, and luckily it's empty. She leads her parents inside and closes the door.

"Meela, was that you in the picture?" Etta Mae asks, her voice sweet and calm.

Her mother's surprised reaction is actually more upsetting than her father's angry one. "Yes but—"

"You said you weren't taking off your clothes," Etta Mae says, confused.

"She obviously lied to us," Clem says.

"I didn't lie. I was paying homage to Josephine Baker in my performance. I came out on stage like that, I didn't remove any of my clothes."

"That cause you ain't wearing any." Clem paces around the small space exasperated.

"Jamila, is that normal? Do you always perform—"

"Naked. The word your momma's looking for is naked," Clem says, still pacing.

Jamila wants to giggle at how comical her father looks being a large man pacing in this tiny room, but she's in enough trouble already.

"I wasn't naked, Daddy."

"You were, damn near."

"Look, I'm sorry I wasn't totally honest with you about what I do here, but I'm not ashamed. I just knew you two would need me to explain it more before you could get on board. I was planning on doing that while you were here, but Daisy ruined that."

"Don't go blaming that little white girl. You had three years to tell us you worked at a place like this and you didn't," Clem snaps.

"A place like what, Daddy?"

"Like what Barry said. It's basically a strip club, and no daughter of mine is working at a place like this."

"Daddy."

"Does your little boyfriend know what goes on here?"

Jamila squares her shoulders and lets out an inpatient breath. While she's tired of her father treating her like a child, she reminds herself to be respectful.

"Yes, Amari was here the night that picture was taken."

"Why am I not surprised?" Clem mutters.

They stay in the dressing room for another twenty minutes to talk, but it's mostly Clem talking and Jamila defending herself. Occasionally, she looks over at Etta Mae, who looks hurt and doesn't say much. When they leave the Kitten Heel, Jamila drives her parents back to the hotel. Everyone agrees that sightseeing is not going to happen, but Etta Mae and Clem are still coming to Vonetta's. And instead of Jamila and Amari picking them up, Clem insists they'll take a Lyft.

Defeated, Jamila agrees and heads back to her car. Just as she gets in, her phone buzzes. She considers not answering it until she notices it's Carly. Maybe she has good news about the three-episode arch on the sitcom Jamila auditioned for.

"Hi, Carly," Jamila tries to sound chipper.

"Meela, are you sitting down?" Carly asks.

Whenever anyone asks if you're sitting down, it's either good news or bad news. "Yeah. I'm sitting in my car," Jamila says, bracing herself for whatever is coming.

"You got it!"

"Oh, my god. I'm going to be on *Twisted Fate*?"

"Better. You got the part of Kandia in *Just an Ordinary Girl*."

"I'm sorry, what?" Jamila is stunned.

"You heard me, babe. The part is yours."

"But I didn't even audition. All I had was a meeting."

"Your little impromptu performance at LaWanda's party, you've had her sold since then. She fought for you, Meela. Her and Kyle and...Amari. He didn't use his cache, but he did let the folks at Echo know how talented you are."

Tears pool in Jamila's eyes. Being with someone who loves her, cherishes her, looks after her, and believes in her is all she's ever wanted. That's all she wanted from Barry, and now she has it in Amari. The stress from her interaction with her parents melts away, and a huge smile spreads across her face. Carly talks some more about contracts and salary. Jamila thanks her profusely and ends the call, calling Amari immediately.

"Hey, baby," he answers.

Jamila can hear the smile in his voice. "I got it, Mar. I'm going to be Kandia."

"I know, Meela. You have no idea how hard it was not to tell you. I'm sorry, but you know I couldn't."

"I know. I understand. Thank you."

"For what?"

"Carly said you, LaWanda, and Kyle fought for me."

"They certainly did. I simply told my bosses that all they needed to do was look at your reel and compare your presence to the other actresses up for the part. They listened, and the rest is history."

"Don't downplay it. You may not have gone as hard as Kyle and LaWanda, but you believed in me enough to convince them to give me a chance."

"I'm always going to believe in you, baby. No matter what."

"I love you so much, Mar," Jamila cries.

"I love you more, Meela."

"Not possible."

"Trust me. It is. Now hurry up and get home to me."

"On my way."

Jamila's smile is a mile wide. This went from being one of the worst days to one of the best days of her life so quickly, her head is spinning. Maybe once her parents hear the good news, they'll forget about the stuff at the Kitten Heel. It's a long shot, but Jamila hopes it will help. If not, she's not sure what she's going to do.

21

AMARI

When Amari and Jamila arrive at Vonetta's, they notice Etta Mae and Clem haven't arrived yet. They both release a sigh of relief. Vonetta comes out of the kitchen and greets them, giving them each a hug.

"Hey, you two!" She looks them over. "Why y'all look like you don't want to be here?"

"It's not that, Momma. Jamila and her parents got into it earlier," Amari explains.

"Why? What happened?"

"They saw the Kitten Heel. More specifically, they saw a picture of me dressed in a banana skirt and not much else."

"Oh, so they don't approve of you working there," Vonetta nods.

"Exactly."

"Well, baby, it's your life, not theirs. You do what you think is best, and don't worry about who judges you. No matter who they are. You hear me?"

"Yes, ma'am."

Twenty minutes later, Tennille and Kenya join them. The vibe is relaxed and chill. Chantel Stone's classic "Kiss Me, Like You Miss Me," plays in the background while Kenya and Tennille set the table and Amari, Jamila, and Vonetta put the finishing touches on dinner. A few more songs belt through the speakers causing Amari to take Jamila by the hand and twirl her into his arms. They slow dance while singing along, Jamila's voice is way better and more polished than his, of course.

"Please, Uncle Pooh. Let Jamila sing."

"Why? What's she got that I don't?" Amari tosses an olive from the crudité platter at Tennille's head.

"Melody," Tennille answers.

"Harmony," Kenya adds.

"Talent," Vonetta yells from the kitchen.

"A voice people actually want to hear," Kenya says, finishing their witty banter.

The ladies all laugh, and Amari shakes his head. Even though he's currently the butt of jokes, Amari is having a wonderful time. It's just like when he and his sisters were younger and they would help their mom make dinner before his father came home from work. There was always light roasting and laughter. Seeing Jamila enjoy herself only makes him more thankful that his mother tricked Mrs. Gordon.

After they make their way back into the kitchen, Amari watches Jamila while she chops veggies. "Can I help you, Mr. Hawkins?"

Wrapping his arms around her waist, Amari kisses Jamila's neck. He loves the way she wears her hair, especially how she has it now, wrapped in a bun, exposing her long delicate neck. Amari boroughs his face in between Jamila's jaw and collar bone.

Jamila giggles. "Remind me to tell you something later."

"What?" Amari kisses her neck some more.

"Mmmm. I'll tell you when we have a moment alone."

"Sounds good."

The doorbell rings, and Amari tenses up.

"Don't worry. I'm the one they're upset with. My dad probably won't even say anything to you."

"That's what I'm afraid of. I don't want him

coming for you either. You say the word, and we'll leave."

"Not after all the trouble your mom went through. It'll be fine, Mar. I swear."

Before Jamila leaves the kitchen to answer the door, Vonetta places a hand on her son's shoulder.

"Don't worry, baby. If they get outta pocket, I'll say something," Vonetta reassures him.

"No need, Momma. If they say anything to Meela, I'll handle it."

The table is set with all kinds of food. Amari and Jamila made her parents' favorite appetizers: potstickers, crab cakes, baby lamb chops, and artichoke dip. For the main course, there's roasted chicken with carrots, potatoes, green beans, freshly baked rolls, and a salad. And for dessert, a no-bake ready-made pie crust and yogurt called strawberry delight since strawberries are Jamila's favorite fruit. The salad and dessert are in the fridge, and dinner is still cooking.

Etta Mae is chatting with Kenya while Tennille gets them something to drink, and Clem helps himself to a crab cake when Vonetta enters.

"Hello! Welcome to our home. It's such a pleasure to finally meet you." Vonetta hugs Clem, then Etta Mae.

"It's nice to meet you, too," Etta Mae replies.

Clem smiles. "These crab cakes are absolutely amazing. You put your foot in these, Ms. Vonetta."

"I'm glad you like them, but I didn't make them. Pooh Bear did."

"Pooh Bear?" Clem asks confused.

"That's what I call my son. Amari made pretty much all the appetizers."

Clem looks over at Amari. He can't tell if the older man is impressed or annoyed. Either way, Clem gives Amari a friendly smile. This must make Jamila nervous because she's chewing on the inside of her jaw. Amari takes her hand and squeezes it. Instantly, he can see the tension leave her body. When Jamila looks at him, he winks.

"Ahem," Clem clears his throat.

"Don't mind them. They do that all the time. These two are always getting lost in each other," Kenya says.

"They are very sweet together," Etta Mae says with a grin.

Thank God! When Jamila told him about how upset her parents were after their visit to the Kitten Heel, Amari wasn't sure they could count on Etta Mae to be an ally anymore. He's never been more grateful to be wrong. The way she's smiling at them tells him she's at least calmed down since this afternoon. Clem, on the other hand, still seems distrustful of Amari and upset with his daughter.

Amari does the only thing he can think of to relax the mood. "May I get you a drink, Mr. Washington?"

"Yes, Johnny Walker black if you have it. On the rocks."

They definitely have it. Amari and Jamila needed this dinner to go well and left no stone unturned.

"I believe we do."

Amari reappears carrying two glasses, one for Clem and one for himself. He hands Clem a glass before taking a sip of his drink. Everyone else is helping themselves to the appetizers and mingling.

"I know that earlier today didn't go as planned, but I hope the remainder of your visit goes better," Amari offers.

"I'm not sure how that's possible. We found out that our daughter is a sex worker in addition to her shacking up with a stranger. Doesn't seem like this trip is salvageable."

"I'm sure that's not true, sir. If you just talk things over with Jamila—"

"We'll talk plenty on the plane."

"I'm sorry. What plane?"

"The plane ride back home tomorrow. Jamila is coming back with us. We talked and we all agree that's what's best."

It's like the wind has been knocked out of Amari's lungs. Is this what Jamila wanted to talk to him about? How could she make such a huge decision without him? She knows all that he went through with Layla. How could she do this? No, Meela wouldn't do this to him. He knows her too well. They love each other too much for it to end like this. Amari takes a breath. Even if she does go back home with her folks, maybe it's to talk her father down. Then when things are good, she'll come back. Yeah, that's it. That has to be it.

Once dinner is ready, everyone makes their way to the table while Vonetta brings out the entrees. Amari knees buckle as he walks to his seat. He gives Jamila a passing glance and she looks alarmed. She mouths, "What's wrong?" But Amari simply shakes his head and walks over to his seat. Amari's so focused on Jamila leaving, he doesn't realize that Clem has already taken it. He's about to sit elsewhere when Vonetta speaks up.

"Clem you're in my son's seat," she says sweetly.

"Oh, I didn't realize the seating was assigned,"

Clem jokes though there is clearly some offense in his tone.

Jamila looks nervously at a saddened Amari.

"It's just that ever since my husband died, Mar has been the man of the house, and that's where his daddy used to sit. It took Mar years to feel comfortable enough to sit there. I don't want him to feel like it's not his place. You understand?"

"If it's that important, I'll move. Besides he looks like he's fin' to start crying any minute." Clem nods.

He switches seats with Amari placing him between Tennille and Vonetta.

"Amari, baby, you do look distressed. What's wrong?" Vonetta asks.

Amari sits down and looks over at Jamila.

"I know what you wanted to tell me, and as hard as it may be, I'm okay with it. Just please promise me that you'll come back to me. I can't have what happened with Layla happen with you. I love you, Meela. I love you so much." Amari clutches Jamila's hand. "Please promise me you'll come back to me."

Jamila looks at him like he has three heads. "Of course, I'm coming back, Mar. I was only going to the store."

Now Amari looks confused. "Wait, what?"

"The store. I'm going to get the ingredients to

make YoYo's famous fried chicken. She finally agreed to give me the recipe, and I'm going to fix it for supper tomorrow."

"What? I mean… What? Why, uh, would you need to wait until we were alone to tell me that?"

"Because YoYo didn't want me to tell Ms. Vonetta."

"Old stingy heffa," Vonetta mutters under her breath.

"What did you think I was going to say?" Jamila asks.

"I thought you were going back to Nebraska with your parents," Amari says with a relieved breath.

"Why on earth would you think that?" Jamila rubs the top of Amari's head.

This is something she started doing when he came home from work stressed. It always works. He feels himself calming down. Her words and the way her hands feel sink in, and Amari closes his eyes and lets out a breath. She's not going, she's staying here with him. When Amari opens his eyes, he glares straight at Clem.

Jamila follows the direction of Amari's glare. "Daddy, what did you do?"

"I simply explained that we would be taking you back home to straighten everything out."

"Clem, how could you?" Etta Mae snaps.

"Etta, you were just as blindsided and upset as I was in that bar."

"I was, but I gave it some thought, and Jamila has always been honest and responsible. There's no sense in holding a grudge. Besides, she's an adult."

"Thank you, Momma." Jamila smiles at her mother and then turns to Clem, her smile fading. "Daddy, you owe everyone here an apology. Ms. Vonetta and her family have done nothing but take good care of me, and they went through a lot of work to make this dinner special for you and Momma. And you especially owe Amari an apology. You have not been fair to him at all. To top it all off, you lied to him. I am not a child. I have a great life here in L.A. and I'm happy. I love my job, my career is taking off, and my man," Jamila looks at Amari lovingly, "is everything I could ask for. I'm not letting anyone take any of those things away from me. Not even you."

Amari looks around the table and doesn't envy Clem. All the women are looking at him, and none of them are happy. Clem shoots Amari a desperate look that says, "Help me out, brother." Amari, in turn, looks away. Clem is on his own.

Clem clears his throat. "I'm sorry. It's hard for a

man to let go of his only child. Especially when that child is a girl. But as you said, you are not a child anymore, and I need to start respecting your decisions. I am sorry everyone. Thank you for looking out for my Meela and…" Clem looks at Amari. "I am sorry, Amari. Jamila loves you and you clearly love her. I won't interfere anymore, or at least I'll try not to."

"Thank you, sir. Now, unless anyone else has any more announcements, let us bow our heads and say grace."

AMARI STANDS IN THE HALLWAY OF HIS FAMILY HOME looking at the framed pictures on the wall, specifically, the one of him and his father when they went on a father/son fishing trip when he was thirteen. They took one every year, and they often did a lot together. His father was his hero, and he taught Mar the importance of being there for people.

"Is that your pops?" Clem asks.

Amari is so deep in thought, he doesn't see Clem slide in next to him. It's a good thing Jamila doesn't see this. She's constantly teasing Mar about his lack of awareness.

"Yes, sir."

"How long ago did he pass?"

"Thirteen years ago."

"What happened? If you don't mind me asking."

"He complained about chest pains and was having trouble breathing. My mom took him to the hospital, and a few days later, he was gone."

"I'm so sorry. Looked like you two were tight."

"We were. We were the only guys in the house. Did you get a chance to talk to my other sisters?"

"Yes, they were nice."

Amari nods and continues, "My dad taught me a lot. Taught me how to be a man." Amari's eyes get glassy.

Clem lets out a breath. "You have a lovely family."

"Thank you."

"Again, I am terribly sorry, Amari. I've misjudged you. I thought you were some slick, rich asshole who saw my baby as a trophy, but I was wrong. You are a good man."

Amari looks at him and smiles. "Thank you again, sir."

"I don't know about you, but I'm ready for some dessert." Clem rubs his belly.

"It should definitely be ready by now."

"You made that too?"

"Yep. Got the recipe from Meela."

"My baby girl can cook. She got that from her momma."

"We are two very lucky men."

"That's no lie, young buck!" Clem says laughing, playfully grabbing Amari by the shoulders.

22

JAMILA

One year later

"And cut! That's a wrap on Jamila Washington," Kyle announces.

The cast and crew applaud. Jamila hugs Kyle and LaWanda, squeezing them tightly. Amari comes up behind her and squeezes her waist. She turns around and hugs him so tight they almost topple over.

"Whoa! I knew you'd be excited to see me, but damn," Amari laughs.

"I didn't think you'd be on set today. You said you had back-to-back meetings."

"You should know by now that I will always make time for you," Amari says, kissing her.

"Aww, Mar, that's so sweet."

"And that's not all, I have a surprise for you. It's in your trailer."

"Give me a few minutes to get out of costume?"

"Sure thing, babe."

Jamila quickly changes to get back to Amari. No makeup, no afro wig, or seventies-era duds. She's much more comfortable in her sweats with her hair pinned up in a bun. She has a new-found respect for actors who go through hours of prosthetics for a role. Wearing a tight-ass wig and platform shoes was killing her. She could only imagine what it was like with literal pounds of makeup and prosthetics on. One of the many things she's grateful for is that Echo didn't cheap out when it came to the wigs, and Amari made sure the hair and makeup team was comprised of Black hairdressers and makeup artists. Too many Black actresses are forced to make do with people who are not familiar with working with people of color. When Jamila mentioned it while talking to YoYo, Amari overheard and made sure that wouldn't be the case on this set. He even went so far as to make changes on the set of *Sisterhood* as well.

"Great work, Jamila," Kyle says squeezing her hand.

"Thank you. I'm going to miss coming to set every day."

"I'm going to miss seeing you all, but don't fret. I'll be seeing you when it's time for ADR."

"True." Jamila smiles.

"Also, there's talk of an Eartha Kitt bio in the works. I'm going to be producing with Samya Warner directing. We'll be working together again in no time."

Jamila's eyes grow to the size of saucers. "Kyle, if you cast me. I will marry you."

"I'm standing right here," Amari complains.

"Hush, baby, we're talking business." Jamila waves Amari off.

Kyle laughs. "No need, Meela. I'll be in touch. See y'all around." Kyle heads over to the DP to go over the last of Jamila's scenes.

She could pinch herself. Now that she's wrapped filming *Just an Ordinary Girl*, she and Amari are taking a much-needed vacation to the Maldives. Then next month, she starts filming *Southpaw*, a western starring Luis Estrada and Robert Emerson where she's playing an outlaw. It's being filmed in a small town an hour outside of L.A. called Northfolk, so Amari is going to be working remotely while being on location with her.

"Are you done drooling over Kyle?" Amari breaks her train of thought.

"Quit pouting, Mar. I wasn't serious."

"Yeah, alright. I shouldn't even give you my surprise anymore. Ungrateful ass."

"Boy, you better quit playing and give me my surprise."

"Fine, but you don't deserve it."

"We'll see about that." Jamila follows Amari, her hand clasped in his.

Finally, they arrive at her trailer. Just as she's about to reach for the door to go in, Amari turns her toward him and smiles. "Close your eyes." Jamila does as she's told, and a door opens. "Okay, open them."

When Jamila opens her eyes, she is surrounded by all the people she loves. Tears form in her eyes as she hugs everyone around her. Her parents, Vonetta, Kenya, Tennille, YoYo, Charmaine, Daisy, and Cleo. Even Iman, Zuri, and their families are here, along with Keith, Erika, and the rest of Amari's crew. She turns to thank Amari when she sees him bent down on one knee.

"Years ago, I told myself I would never do this again. I told myself that I was better off being alone. Love wasn't worth the risk of being hurt. You proved me wrong, time and time again. I love you so much, Meela. We don't always agree—Bear Burgers are good but they are not the best burgers in L.A.—"

"They are," Jamila argues.

"Woman, please. Even In N Out is better." Everyone laughs, wiping away tears. "The point is, no matter where we land on anything, I hope it will always be together. You made my house a home, and you've made me so unbelievably happy and fulfilled, more than I ever thought I could be. Marry me, Meela." Amari reveals a pink diamond engagement ring to her. "I want us to spend the rest of our lives taking care of each other."

Jamila's crying so hard, she can barely breathe. Cleo, Charmaine, and Daisy playfully nudge her.

"Girl, you better say yes. That's Harry Winston on your finger," Charmaine teases.

"If she says no, I'll marry you, Mar," Cleo winks.

"Me too. Cleo, we can be sister-wives," Daisy cheers.

"That works for me," Cleo says.

"Okay, okay. Enough of that," Jamila says, playfully frowning before she turns to Amari. "So, you thought I didn't deserve this surprise, huh?"

"I mean, I guess you do. Besides, I already went through all the trouble getting people here, having

Bree reschedule some things, writing, and delivering that speech—"

"It was a damn good speech," Jamila says sniffling.

"Hell yeah, it was." They both laugh.

"What do you say, Ms. Washington? Would you like to become Mrs. Hawkins?"

Jamila pulls Amari's hands, urging him to stand. When he does, she gazes into his eyes.

"Yes."

Everyone applauds and cheers as Jamila kisses Amari and hugs him for the longest before they break apart. He slips the ring on her finger, a huge smile on his face as he does.

"Alright, y'all let's head out. The 'She Said Yes' party is at Szechuan Garden!" Vonetta announces. Everyone heads out following Vonetta.

Jamila giggles.

"What's so funny?" Amari asks.

"What would have happened if I said no?"

"Then this would be a very awkward party."

"You still would have had it?"

"After I made that deposit to rent out the whole restaurant? Damn right. It just would have been a 'She Said No, Come Watch Mar Get Drunk as He Eats His Weight in Eggrolls' party."

Jamila bursts out laughing and loops her arm around Amari's, leaning into him.

"I love you, Mar."

"I love you, too, baby. I'm so happy you're going to be mine forever."

"I always was."

www.ingramcontent.com/pod-product-compliance
Lightning Source LLC
Chambersburg PA
CBHW051427130726
47987CB00005B/1949